"You're not a gracious loser, Mimi."

"No one likes to lose, Chase."

Some of the fire went out of her voice, though. He looked genuinely relaxed and happy and it was hard not to replicate. It was obvious from the faint lines between his dark eyebrows that he typically worried more than he relaxed.

"I wish things hadn't ended so poorly between us, Mimi."

"So do I," she admitted.

His head was tilted at almost exactly the right angle for a kiss. Not that she should be kissing Chase Ferguson, but if he leaned in...oh yes, she'd kiss him. She'd kiss the life out of him, if for no other reason than to learn if her lips still fitted against his like they were made to.

* * *

A Snowbound Scandal is part of the
Dallas Billionaires Club series
from Jessica Lemmon!

Dear Reader,

Forced proximity is my favorite trope in romance! When I planned Chase Ferguson's story, I wanted two things: a reunion with a woman he'd left behind and an unrelenting blizzard that trapped them together. Even better? I set the book in Montana, in the drop-dead gorgeous mansion Chase visits when he's not busy with his mayoral duties back in Dallas. The heroine, Miriam, is stubborn and willful, but above all else, she's *kind*. She cares too much. So much, that fiercely protective Chase made the mistake of letting her go ten years ago rather than handing her his heart.

From fireside chats to soaking in the indoor hot tub to bonding over gooey grilled-cheese sandwiches, we experience Chase and Miriam reconciling their past with the present, one step at a time. They soon uncover that as different as they are, they still feel the same about each other a decade later. It took a few sizzling encounters for them to realize that beneath their strong physical attraction was real and lasting *love*.

Grab a cup of hot cocoa and settle in. I hear there's snow in the forecast—a lot of it.

Happy reading!

Jessica Lemmon

JESSICA LEMMON

A SNOWBOUND SCANDAL

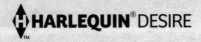

Recycling programs
for this product may
not exist in your area.

ISBN-13: 978-1-335-97167-8

A Snowbound Scandal

HARLEQUIN®
www.Harlequin.com

Printed in U.S.A.

A former job-hopper, **Jessica Lemmon** resides in Ohio with her husband and rescue dog. She holds a degree in graphic design currently gathering dust in an impressive frame. When she's not writing supersexy heroes, she can be found cooking, drawing, drinking coffee (okay, wine) and eating potato chips. She firmly believes God gifts us with talents for a purpose, and with His help, you can create the life you want.

Jessica is a social media junkie who loves to hear from readers. You can learn more at jessicalemmon.com.

Books by Jessica Lemmon

Harlequin Desire

Dallas Billionaires Club
Lone Star Lovers
A Snowbound Scandal

Visit her Author Profile page at Harlequin.com, or jessicalemmon.com, for more titles!

For John.
There's no one I'd rather be
snowed in with than you.

One

Mayor Chase Ferguson's best friend and head of his security team strolled into his office, sheet of paper in hand.

"Busy?" Emmett asked.

"Extremely," Chase answered, droll. He'd been staring at the same spot on the wall for going on twenty minutes trying to figure out how to answer the governor's email.

"I won't be long." Emmett wasn't smiling, but Chase could tell his best bud was amused. Emmett knew Chase better than anyone—better than his own family in some cases. With a flick of his fingers, Emmett dropped the sheet of paper on the desk.

Chase lifted the printed color photo. In it, a delicate, thin woman, mouth open in an angry shout was holding a poster board. On the poster was a photo of a bird dripping with black goo and the words painted around the image read OIL KILLS. An angry crowd in the background held similar signs, but it was the woman in clear focus that snared his attention.

Soft, dark curls blew over fine cheekbones and plump lips. Even now, years later, he didn't have to try to recall the feel of her elegant, slim body against his. Mimi Andrix was runway-model thin with small breasts and subtle curves. The years had been good to her, depending on how recently this photo was taken.

"When was it taken?" Chase asked.

"Three years ago, in Houston."

"How did you come across it?"

"One of your campaign staff alerted me. It was mailed to the office alongside a letter threatening to send it to Jamie Holland."

Chase's opponent. An all around `not-so-nice guy with questionable ties to big, bad men in Texas, and involved in too many illegal activities to list.

"We're trying to find out where it's from, but so far no luck," Emmett said in the same flat, matter-of-fact tone.

Chase grunted. Ah, election season. He was on his second term and preferred to stay where he was for as long as his city allowed him. Not only was he one of Dallas's youngest mayors, but he was also one of the few politicians interested in the seat who was unbribable. As a son of the Fergusons and one-third owner of Ferguson Oil, Chase had plenty of money of his own. He didn't crave power or prestige. He craved justice. Staying in office meant crowding out potentially corrupt politicians. Jamie Holland, for example.

"I recognized her right away." Emmett tapped the edge of the photo. He'd been on the three-month-long trip where Chase had met Mimi. Emmett was one of the few people who knew what had transpired between them all those summers ago. All that had gone well before it'd gone sideways.

"She should know that she's a potential target for publicity." Mimi hated politics. She wouldn't appreciate being dragged into the mud during his upcoming campaign if and when news of their previous relationship saw the light of day.

"I tracked her down. She lives in Bigfork. You have a trip scheduled for Montana soon, don't you? Why not tell her in person?" His friend smirked knowingly.

"Somehow I doubt she'd welcome me with open arms." The last time Chase had seen her, he'd put her on a plane leaving Dallas for Bigfork. Her face was red from a combination of anger and devastation—both of which he'd put into her expression. She'd hated him then and he doubted her feelings for him had warmed since.

"She works for a conservation society. Some environmental group. Her bio on the website mentioned 'saving the planet.'"

That drew a proud smile to Chase's mouth. Mimi's giving and loving heart had been so huge it'd encapsulated not only him, but the environmental causes she'd cared about so passionately. Not until she'd come with him to Dallas did she know the extent of Chase's involvement in *one of the biggest enemies to the environment*— her words. The oil industry was his family's industry.

But she didn't call it quits between them when she found out. Chase was surprised she'd seen around his inherited billions that had come from the very industry destroying the causes she'd championed, but she had. She'd tearfully told him she didn't hold it against him and that they'd work through it and that the only thing that mattered was how they felt for each other.

He'd been the one who'd ended it. It'd killed him to do it. Even though they never would've worked out, he'd cared about her and would've preferred ending their relationship on better terms.

"Do you ever wonder," Emmett said as he turned for the door, "if you two had married how that would've gone?"

"No." Chase never second-guessed decisions. The point of making one was that you didn't have to revisit it.

"Seeing that photo made me wonder if she'd have bent to your will and become a proper politician's wife, or if you would've caved to hers and been alongside her protesting the evils of big oil."

The bagel Chase had for breakfast turned to stone in his stomach. He didn't like thinking about what would've happened. What could've happened.

What a colossal waste of resources.

"The first one," he answered. Which was exactly why he hadn't continued a relationship with Mimi. She was too good at being who she was to be dragged into politics, having to explain herself or apologize for her past. Chase's desire to protect her had dominated his decision to put her on that airplane. Clean breaks were best, and he'd told her as much at the time.

Emmett shut the door behind him, leaving Chase in his office with thoughts he didn't care to have. He'd had plenty of brief relationships in the ten years since he and Mimi had ended theirs. He didn't know if it was the age they'd been at the time—him twenty-six to her twenty-three—or if it'd been the high of a summer fling, but she stood out in his mind to this day. The rare act of being wrapped in her arms for three months had felt more like three years.

Whatever it was, she'd left a mark. An indelible one.

Back then, he hadn't been as conservative as he was now. He'd been more like his father, Rider. With a rough edge. His mother, Eleanor, had taken it upon herself to sand those edges down on her boys. It'd worked on Chase, and while Zach fell into line with the company, his wild streak was still strong. Chase's had been buried long ago. Hell, it was probably on the bottom of Flathead Lake in Montana.

Once he'd become certain of his political interests, he'd gladly gone from rough to refined. If he hadn't gone the refined route, he imagined he'd have turned out like Emmett, who was best described as rough on the edges *and* in the middle. Emmett had started out in security—a perfect fit for his bulk and brawn— and it wasn't long before Chase had asked him to run his security detail.

Emmett was still in charge of security, but his duties now spanned anything that had to do with Chase's position as mayor. Loyalty was the one luxury you couldn't buy in the world of politics, so Chase considered himself lucky that a lifelong friend had his back.

He lifted the photo again and tried to imagine himself with Mimi today. It'd been ten years since he'd seen her—since he'd said goodbye. She'd accused him of being a coward. Of being too obtuse to see what she'd seen so clearly. She'd stood on the airfield before boarding the private plane and shouted over the whining engine that they loved each other and were the kind of couple who could last forever.

If you give us a chance.

He hadn't, though.

Chase pulled the lap drawer on his desk open and locked the photo inside. Despite Mimi's passionate argument, he'd known then that they couldn't know if they'd last forever after only a handful of months. No matter how good the sex had been or the way the minutes had folded over into hours and rolled into days and morphed into months.

The smile that found his face now wasn't one of regret, but of memory. The weeks and months before their bitter end had been filled with Mimi's laugh and her fingers ruffling his hair. He recalled the way she sighed in his ear, hot and quiet, when he made love to her. She'd dragged him to the lake on more than one occasion, torn off her clothes and his, and talked him into skinny-dipping in the full moon's light.

Hopefully no photos of those nights resurfaced next.

Yes, he had a lot of good memories from that summer. Like the time they had sneaked onto a massive property overlooking the lake. The house was disgustingly arrogant in its placement and had boasted shamelessly from its many windowed rooms.

Eight bedrooms. Six bathrooms. Fifteen thousand square feet.

He knew because he'd kept a close eye on the property over the years, waiting on the elusive owner to die or move out.

The owner had put the mansion up for sale three years ago, and Chase purchased it for a cool sixteen mil. It'd been completely remodeled by then. During his walk-through he'd been awestruck by the fact that the inside was more immaculate and braggadocian than the outside. Multiple fireplaces, a hot tub alongside an indoor heated pool surrounded by huge rocks and a wine cellar to name a few of the amenities.

With the purchase of the mansion he also became owner of a good slice of the Flathead Lake shoreline. Since he'd purchased the place he'd been there three—no, *four*—times. He tried to visit once a year, minimum. During those trips, thoughts of Mimi didn't cling to him like moss on a rock, but passed by like a leaf on the surface of a stream. He didn't linger on memory or the past. What was the point?

He stood from his desk to take in the city outside his office window. Dallas sat fat and happy, calm and cooling down for autumn. He was eighteen months out from reelection, and though reelection efforts were always in swing, they wouldn't be in *full* swing for a while.

His scheduled trip to Bigfork was likely his last chance to flee town, to untangle himself from the political spider web for a bit. If the worst happened—if Mimi became embroiled in political mudslinging, it'd be best if he were here in Dallas, not in her backyard.

He contemplated skipping the trip for all of two seconds. He could handle the press—good or bad. It's how he'd been elected. He wasn't shying away from the trip because of Mimi, nor was he going there for her.

The past was the past and the future was all that mattered.

Decision made.

Bigfork, here he came.

"Honestly, Stefanie." Eleanor Ferguson tsked her only daughter from across the dining room table.

Stefanie rolled her eyes. Her mother tended to bring out the child in her. Probably because she was treated like one whenever they gathered for holidays. Or a *pseudo*holiday like this one.

She slid a glance over at her brothers. Chase, in a suit and tie, fresh from working late, sat rigidly in his chair. He hoisted one regal eyebrow at her but otherwise stayed silent. Zach sat next to his wife, Penelope, but he was too preoccupied with his ten-month-old daughter to pay attention to his bickering mother and sister.

The other party at the table wasn't family at all. Emmett Keaton, Chase's head of security and best friend, sat at the head of the table opposite her father. He silently ate a few forked green beans and watched her, expressionless as per his usual.

God, he made her *crazy*.

He'd been breathing down her neck since that unfortunate run-in with one of Chase's sworn political enemies. Emmett had watched over her like a hawk since. She'd been so aware of his presence lately, she looked forward to any event that didn't include him. Yet here he was.

"This doesn't count as Thanksgiving," Stef dropped her napkin on her empty plate and her mother, who'd been insisting she take the serving spoon, dropped it back into the mashed potatoes with a sigh.

The chef-prepared meal—Mom didn't cook—was top-notch. Golden, buttery turkey, stuffing, French green beans, and a gravy boat brimming with brown gravy. There was only one problem.

"Thanksgiving isn't for another two weeks. This is just..." Stef shook her head. "Wrong."

Emmett grunted what might've been a laugh and she sliced him with a glare. He shoveled another bite into his mouth and chewed.

"Why is he here?" she asked the table collectively.

"Rider. Remind your daughter she is to have manners in this house." Elle looked over at her husband.

"Stef, sweetheart." Her dad smiled. "We're all making sacrifices. You think I want to be on a boat during my favorite holiday of the year?"

"It's a *cruise*," her mom corrected.

"Em's here because he can't turn down a free meal," Chase said conversationally.

Emmett grunted again. Stef guessed that was his way of agreeing with his friend.

Neanderthal.

"It doesn't seem right for everyone to leave during Thanksgiving." Sacrilegious, even, but she didn't want to be melodramatic. But honestly, did tradition mean nothing to anyone but her? Chase was vacationing at a lake in Montana by himself; Zach and Pen were traveling with their daughter Olivia to visit Pen's parents in Chicago, which was, *okay, fine*, excusable; and her parents were going to be floating in the Atlantic Ocean wearing bathing suits and drinking mai tais.

"I'll be here," Emmett offered.

"Lucky me." Stefanie mimicked his sarcastic smile and he went back to his food. She'd rather eat a micro-waved frozen meal by herself than take him up on a shared turkey-day dinner.

"Stef, my parents would love to have you if you want to come to Chicago with us." Pen lifted her fuss-ing daughter from the high chair. Zach shot his wife a look that said they hadn't talked about this.

Her brother's wife was sweet and thoughtful and sharp and beautiful. If Zach hadn't pulled his head from his rear and married Pen, Stef would've seri-ously considered it. Penelope Ferguson had granted them all a beautiful niece-slash-granddaughter, and Pen's presence at parties made Stef's life a lot brighter. As much as she'd love to hang with Pen over the holi-days, however, Stef would never dream of intruding on Pen's time with her family. This would be their first Thanksgiving with Olivia.

"I appreciate that," Stef smiled over at her sister-in-law. "But I'll be all right. I'll just…decorate for Christmas early."

"You mean late," Zach said. "You barely waited until Halloween last year before you adorned every-thing that crossed your path in red, green and gold."

Stef curled her lip at her brother. Zach smirked.

"If you change your mind, let us know." Pen ex-cused herself from the table to take care of Olivia and Zach stood with her.

"Need help?"

"No, I have her." She kissed him and he smiled, adoration on his face.

So. Stinking. Sweet.

"I'm not inviting you to Montana." Chase scooped more mashed potatoes onto his plate. "So don't ask."

"I don't want to spend Thanksgiving with you, anyway," she teased.

He pointed at her with his fork when he said, "Good."

Her oldest brother had always looked out for her, had always been there for her. She could guarantee if she wanted to abscond to Montana with Chase, he wouldn't hesitate taking her along. But he deserved a break, too. There'd been so much fatigue in his eyes tonight. Must've been a hell of a week in the mayor's office.

"How are you spending the holiday, Emmett?" Elle asked.

"I'll be on call. Security never sleeps."

Stef eyed him over the rim of her water glass, trying to decide if that was true or not. She didn't know Emmett that well, only that he and Chase had been friends for years, and that Emmett was part of the backdrop of nearly every big event in recent history. She assumed that behind those hulking shoulders and permanent scowl of his, she'd find a loner who worked 24/7, and not much else. He didn't seem to have a life other than one involving the Ferguson family.

Not five minutes later, Penelope returned without Olivia, explaining her daughter had missed a nap and was too tired to deal with dinner.

"It's Zach's turn so I'm off the clock." She refilled her wineglass with dark red wine and gestured to Stef with the tipped bottle. "Join me?"

"Always." Stef allowed Pen to fill her glass, feeling a ping of loneliness. Stef was used to her family being around, to big parties and to-dos year-round. Save when Zach had lived in Chicago for a stint, they'd been together as a family most of the time. The business they held stakes in kept them in each other's orbit.

So, yeah, Stef wasn't used to being alone, but that didn't mean she couldn't be. This year she'd embrace Thanksgiving on her own and build that muscle.

It was time her family started seeing her as a twenty-nine-year-old anyway.

Two

Bundled in her knee-length pea coat, Miriam Andrix marched up the asphalt-covered parking lot, her
head down to thwart the icy wind. She was born and
raised in Montana, but every winter she experienced
here made her a bit less tolerant of the cold. Which
was ridiculous. She was only thirty-three, for Pete's
sake. It wasn't as if she was her seventy-five-year-old
grandmother who kept the thermostat set on eighty
degrees at home.

She peeked up from her trudge so that she didn't
mow over a shopper who'd just overspent on groceries,
and then tucked her chin again and watched her
laced boots move her forward. Her destination? Whole
Foods Market in search of fixings for sweet potato
pie, as assigned by her mother. This was the first year
Miriam had been placed in charge of dessert. Typi-

cally, she made a side dish like potatoes au gratin or cranberry sauce.

Mom's rules were anything but simple when asking her four children to participate in the preparation of Thanksgiving dinner: no canned ingredients, organic if you can. She also provided the family recipe cards for the requested dish—tweaked by each generation to add an extra dash of cinnamon here or an additional crushed garlic clove there. And since Miriam was responsible for a dessert she wasn't comfortable making, she wasn't taking any chances on shopping at the corner market. She might well spend her entire paycheck in here, but at least she could guarantee that only the most beautiful sweet potatoes would go into her pie.

At the entrance of Whole Foods, the automated doors swished aside and the fragrant scent of mulled cider wafted out. She lifted her head and closed her eyes to inhale her most favorite scent—autumn—when a competing smell mingled with the cider.

Sandalwood. Pine. A touch of leather… And eerily familiar. As was the voice that crashed into her like a runaway shopping cart.

"Mimi?"

She snapped her head up and her gaze collided with a man taller than her by several inches, his devastatingly handsome face broken up by the frown on his forehead and additional lines at the corners of his gray-green eyes. His jaw sported a barely-there five o'clock shadow, and his hair was in the same disarray she remembered from ten years ago—the one crooked part of Chase Ferguson that couldn't be tamed.

"Chase. Hi." She blinked again at the man in front of her, having the half-crazed thought that she'd summoned him with her mind. A week ago she'd received a photo of herself in an envelope she'd had to sign for. Along with the photo was a letter from the mayor of Dallas's office—Chase's office—that was signed by a woman's hand. Miriam had read the two neatly typed paragraphs and tossed the letter into the trash. There was no action step for her, merely a "making you aware" note that she might be mentioned in Mayor Chase Ferguson's upcoming campaign and "may be called upon in the future" for her cooperation.

But throwing the letter into the wastebasket hadn't removed the memories of Chase from her head. For a solid week, she'd reflected on the summer they'd spent together, fumed anew at the senseless way he'd cast her aside and played out a few scenarios wherein she'd enjoy humiliating his mother—whom Miriam blamed in part for Chase breaking things off.

"I didn't expect to run into you while I was here," the man from her past was saying. It was the same deep, silken voice she remembered, but his Texas drawl was diminished, no doubt due to rigorous training from a speech coach.

"That's my line," she said with a flat smile, stepping aside to allow a woman pushing a stroller to go in ahead of her.

Chase palmed Miriam's arm and physically moved her to the side of the automated door, and if she was still twenty-three and over-the-moon crazy about him, she might have said that his hand was warm and brought back memories of the summer they spent with each other, most of those days wearing as little clothing as was legal. Sometimes less.

"Yes, I suppose that would be your line." His smile

hitched at one corner and dropped like it'd never been there. He adjusted the paper grocery bag in the crook of his arm.

"What are you doing in Montana?" She had to ask. Because seriously—*what*?

"My annual break from the political hoopla."

Annual?

A brisk wind cut through her coat and she pulled her shoulders under her ears. "I received a letter mentioning said hoopla."

"Good. It's only fair for you to know. We suspect someone on my opponent's camp dug that photo up." He sounded so distant standing not a foot away from her. The same way the letter had sounded—probably because it'd been written by a member of his staff and not Chase himself. Too many years had passed for that to hurt, but part of her had felt the sting of loss that he hadn't bothered with a personal note.

"Where are you staying?"

"I have a place here."

"You do?" News to her.

"On Flathead Lake."

Another memory hit her—one of her cajoling him into skinn-dipping in that lake. On the shoreline on private property in the middle of a warm July night. The water had been cold despite the calendar's date, but Miriam had talked him into it. Watching Chase undress and dive in ahead of her had been one of the highlights of her summer. He had a great ass.

She studied his broad shoulders and tall form, feeling that same commanding presence now. The pull he had on her might have shrunk, but he sure hadn't. If anything, he'd grown both physically and figuratively.

Hell, he was as big as Texas in a way—in charge of part of the gargantuan state with a billionaire fortune in his back pocket.

"Pinecone Drive," he said as if he'd been waiting to share that bit of intel.

"You don't mean…the house on the hill with all the windows?" She adjusted her purse strap on her shoulder as the doors swished open again. More cinnamon smells assaulted her and tempted her into the warmth, out of the brisk wind and away from the physical reminder of the summer fling that had gone from scorching hot to corpse cold in three months' time.

"One and the same. I bought it a few years back. I always liked the way it looked. I don't visit much, unfortunately."

"And now you're here with…your family?" *Wife? Kids?* she thought but didn't add.

"Alone. My parents are going on a cruise to Barbados and my brother Zach and his wife and their daughter are spending the holiday in Chicago."

"Zach's married." She smiled at the idea of Chase's younger brother married with a child. She'd only met him once, but had warm memories of the smiling blond guy with green eyes. Chase's younger sister had been fresh out of high school at the time but Miriam had met her too, in passing. "And Stefanie?"

"She's good. Single. It's good for her."

"Yeah. It's good for me, too," Miriam couldn't help saying.

"For me, as well."

They had a mini standoff, meeting each other's gazes for a few seconds. In that protracted moment, she could feel a whisper of the past roll over them. It spoke of what could've been if they'd stayed together instead of separated. What would've been if... So many ifs.

Miriam tore her gaze away from him and looked through the glass doors at the cornucopia of produce waiting to greet her. She'd be safe in there. Safe from her past snuggling up and threatening to suffocate her. Standing next to Chase made her want to simultaneously move closer and back away.

A defense mechanism, no doubt.

"I'd better get going. I have to buy ingredients for sweet potato pies for my family's Thanksgiving."

"My favorite."

"It is?"

"But I couldn't find it in the freezer section, so..." Chase reached into the grocery bag and pulled out a frozen cherry pie, then from behind it a frozen pizza.

"You can't be serious. Pizza for Thanksgiving dinner?"

"I have wine at the house, too. I can be fancy."

He was "fancy" incarnate. From his shiny shoes to the expensive suit hiding under a long, dark coat. A tie was cinched at his neck just so. He smelled of wealth and warmth. It was harder to imagine him eating a meal that came from a box than it was to picture him pouring wine from a bottle with a thousand-dollar price tag.

"If frozen pizza sounds too labor-intensive, I may go the route of grilled cheese," he said. "I have a loaf of sourdough and three types of cheddar in this bag." He offered a brief smile. She watched his frowning forehead relax and a hint of levity tickle his lips. The transformation kicked her in the stomach. In that brief half of a second Chase had looked years younger. *Ten years* younger to be precise. He'd reminded her of the boy she'd fallen in love with.

And oh, how she'd fallen. So hard that if she'd broken bones it'd have been less painful than the broken heart she'd suffered. He hadn't been there to catch her. He'd simply stepped out of the way.

"Well. Enjoy your bread and cheese, in whichever form you choose." She offered a curt nod, and without ending the conversation gracefully, turned away.

"Mimi, wait." A masculine hand shot out in front of her, his arm brushing hers as he offered a business card. His deep voice rumbled in her ear, "My personal cell number if you have any issues. Any at all."

She swallowed thickly before accepting the card. Then nodded, and, without looking back, dashed into the grocery. She skipped the temptation of a cider with whipped cream at the cafe, terrified that any delay might prompt Chase to follow her in and resume their stilted conversation.

A conversation that had no place in the current year. A conversation that could only end in an argument since she and Chase were on the opposite sides of many, many topics.

Not the least of which was the state of her heart when she'd boarded a plane that long-ago summer.

She stopped at the display of sweet potatoes, but there were only two knobby yams left. She clucked her tongue at her timing, which couldn't be worse. Both for sweet potato shopping and running into ex-boyfriends who should look a lot less tempting.

The simple black-and-white business card weighed

heavy in her hand but she couldn't part with it just yet. She shoved it into her purse and instead debated her next step. Either bribe the woman next to her into relinquishing a few of her sweet potatoes or buy the damn things in a can and hope to God her mother didn't notice.

Three

"Kristine Andrix. Saver of the day!" her youngest sister announced as she strode into Miriam's apartment the next evening. Kristine placed a handled paper sack on the counter and Miriam peeked inside, gawking at the gorgeous produce within.

"Oh, they're beautiful!"

"And organic. I bought them last week since I started eating sweet potatoes for breakfast."

"Breakfast?" Ever the health nut, Kris was always up to some culinary experiment or another. Last year she was vegan and brought her own Tofurkey to Thanksgiving dinner; this year she was vegetarian but only ate "whole foods."

"Yeah. You bake the potato ahead of time, then in the morning pull it out of the fridge, warm it and top it with peanut butter and cinnamon."

"That…actually sounds delicious." Miriam moved to the sink to scrub the spuds. "What time are you driving to mom's tomorrow?"

"I'm going tonight."

"Tonight?" So much for the wine she'd picked up. She was hoping they could share a glass while she regaled her sister with the tale of the Billionaire Mayor in Bigfork.

"Brendan and I were invited to stay the night." She waggled her eyebrows.

"In the same room?"

"Crazy, right? Dad never would've allowed it." Kris's mouth pulled into a sad smile. They all missed him so much. The holidays were the hardest. "I think Wendy helped lighten up the entire household."

"Yes, all it took was her bringing Rosalie home for Christmas."

"Mom prides herself in being progressive."

"I'm bummed, though. I was hoping we could polish off a bottle of wine like we used to…" Miriam decided not to add the words "before Brendan" to that statement. She wouldn't rob her sister of her happiness. She placed the washed potatoes on a pan and Kristine started stabbing them with a fork.

"Why not go tonight?" Kris lived in Bigfork, not too far from Miriam.

"I have work to do. A report that should've been done earlier this week."

"Seems unfair for you to work on the biggest drinking day of the year." Her sister quirked her lips.

"Well, I'm staying Thanksgiving night so that we can raid the stores at the crack of dawn on the biggest *shopping* day of the year."

"Too bad you're not still dating Gerard. Brendan would've had someone to talk to."

"Gerard wasn't a great talker." It'd been the reason they split. He hardly shared anything about his life, little or big. How his workday went, his plans for the weekend or the fact that he'd been seeing another woman at the same time he'd dated Miriam. His silence had been absolute on that front. "We have a horrible track record of having boyfriends at the same time, don't we?"

"The worst."

Kristine and Miriam were ten months apart. Their older siblings Ross and Wendy had a six- and four-year gap on Miriam, respectively. Given that the two youngest Andrix daughters had never *not* remembered the other being around, Kristine and Miriam felt more like twins. They shared the same wavy dark hair that curled on the ends, and had similar full-lipped pouts. Kristine was built more like Wendy, though, on the curvier side, whereas Miriam couldn't do enough leg exercises to thicken her spindles into anything resembling *curves*.

"Speaking of boyfriends…" Potatoes wrapped in foil, Miriam slid the tray into the oven. She set the timer and then leaned on the counter while Kristine poured herself a glass of water from the pitcher. "I ran into Chase Ferguson at Whole Foods."

Mouth agape, Kris blinked. "Come again?"

"I was walking in and he was walking out. He's on vacation. I guess he bought the estate on Pinecone Drive."

"The one with the indoor pool and the wine cellar and a million bedrooms?"

"Uh-huh. And fifteen thousand square feet over-looking Flathead Lake."

"Wow." Kris's eyes sought the ceiling in awe, then jerked back to Miriam. "You seem awfully calm about this."

"I've had a few hours to cope."

"You were so in love with him." Kris shook her head in a pitying fashion. "Like, *gone*."

"Yes, thank you for that reminder."

"What'd he look like?"

"Oh, you know. Tall, dark and handsome."

"Ouch." Her sister winced. "Who's he here with?"

"No one. Not a single soul."

"Really…because his wife and kids are in a Tuscan villa on holiday while he's here writing his memoirs?"

"There is no wife. There are no kids," Miriam said. "At least I don't think there are any kids. We didn't get past him mentioning he was single."

"Sounds like you two had quite the conversation." Her sister deftly raised one eyebrow.

"We mostly stood shivering in the cold while try-ing to find the balance between polite and concise. His parents and siblings are going out of town over Thanksgiving weekend, so he came here to enjoy his rarely used mansion and eat frozen pizza instead." Miriam fingered the bent corner of the recipe card her mother had given her. "He said sweet potato pie was his favorite. I never knew that. Do you know why?"

"I'm assuming because in the short summer months you two spent boinking each other in the lake, you never broached the topic of pie preferences?"

"Fair point." Miriam smiled. "I was going to say it's because we ended before sweet potato pie season.

It's been ages since I've thought about him… I mean
really thought about him. It was a silly summer fling
and I was swept up." Her gut pinged with warning at
the lie. Miriam ignored that ping. She would rather
make believe she never loved him than consider that
she'd been right about them living happily ever after
if he hadn't discarded her so callously. Half kidding,
she added, "I could invite him to Mom's for dinner.
Bury that axe for good."

"Do it."

She faced her sister's wide-eyed gaze. "What?
Why? I was joking."

"Burying the axe for good would be cathartic. Once
you're around each other again you'll both see that
you are *not* the Miriam of ten years ago. You're the
Miriam of today. It'd do Chase good to see what he's
been missing."

"Thanks, Kris." Miriam was touched, but not sure
she agreed. "He's not missing much. Other than a job
I love, I have no husband, children or Nobel Peace
Prize to wave in his face."

"None of that matters." Kristine swept Miriam's
cell phone off the dining room table and offered it, but
then frowned. "Unless… You probably don't have his
private number. I didn't think about that."

"Actually, I do. He handed me his card."

"Bury the lead why don't you! Why'd he give you
that?" Kris was grinning, her eyes twinkling. "For
like, a holiday hookup?" She blinked, then screwed
her eyes toward the ceiling. "That'd be a great book
title."

Her sister the freelance editor never shut her brain off.

"It would be a great title *for a work of fiction*." Miriam snatched her phone away and shoved it into her back pocket. "Remember that protest I did years ago with a conservation group in Houston?"

"Big oil, right?"

Miriam nodded and explained the letter that'd arrived last week. "He didn't plan on seeing me while he was here, so I don't know what the offer of calling him if I need anything was about."

"Told you. Holiday hookup." Her sister shrugged. "You should invite him for no other reason than we can skewer him at the dinner table about being a dirty politician while you're the Snow White of Bigfork."

Miriam had to laugh at her sister's imagination.

"Plus, it'd be fun to watch Mom go from simmer to boiling over while she tries to make sense of a mayor at her table."

"It was a dumb idea. Forget I mentioned it." Miriam just hadn't liked the thought of him alone on a holiday. How ridiculous was that? She wasn't in charge of his well-being.

"Spoilsport."

Topic dead, they went back to chatting about everything but sexy mayors and summer flings.

Two hours later, the pies had finished baking and were cooling on the stovetop. Miriam had poured herself a glass of red after Kristine left, and camped out on the sofa, laptop and charts spread on the coffee table for work. But the website she'd pulled up had nothing to do with work. It was the City of Dallas website, particularly Chase's headshot. He looked merely handsome in that still frame. He'd been devastatingly gorgeous in person.

Chase's business card in hand, she rubbed her thumb over his phone number.

One glass of wine was all it took to weaken her resolve. That and the smell of sweet potato pie in the air.

"Damn him."

She swiped the screen of her phone, dialed the first eight digits of the phone number, then paused.

Why should she care if her ex-boyfriend ate alone on Thanksgiving? Shouldn't she embrace the idea of the jerk who broke her heart spending the holiday alone in a way-too-big-for-one mansion? Except she'd always been horrible at holding grudges, and even the blurry, faded memories of her broken heart couldn't keep her from completing the task.

She dialed the remaining digits and waited patiently while the phone rang once, twice and then a third time. When she was about to give up, a silken voice made love to her ear canal.

"Chase Ferguson."

"Chase. Hi. Um, hi. It's Miriam."

"Miriam?"

"Andrix," she said through clenched teeth. Was it that he'd had so many other women in his life over the last decade that he couldn't keep track of them? Or was it that he'd forgotten her already even though she'd bumped into him yesterday afternoon?

"I know. I think of you as Mimi."

That husky voice curled around her like a hug. He'd always called her Mimi, and to date had been the only person who had, save her best friend in the third grade. Her family either called her Miriam or Meems.

"Is everything all right?" If that was concern in his voice, she couldn't place it. His tone was even. His words measured.

"Everything is fine. I, um." She cleared her throat,

took a fortifying sip of her wine and continued. "My mother lives about twenty minutes north of Bigfork. We make enough for Thanksgiving dinner to feed ten extra people. You're welcome to join us tomorrow night."

She pressed her lips together before she rattled off what would be served and how she'd baked two pies that were presumably his favorite. She wasn't begging him to show up, simply extending an invitation as an old acquaintance.

Silence greeted her from the other end of the phone.

"Chase?"

"No. Thank you."

She waited for an explanation. None came. Not even a lame excuse about having to work like she'd used tonight. Though she truly did have to work. She scowled at her laptop and his handsome mug before snapping the lid shut.

"Will there be anything else?" he asked. Tersely.

At his formal tone, ire slipped into her bloodstream as stealthily as a drug. Her back went ramrod straight; her eyebrows crashed down.

"No," she snapped. "That concludes my business with you."

"Very well."

She waited for goodbye but he didn't offer one. So she hung up on him.

"Jerk." She tossed the phone on the coffee table and rose to refill her glass. She'd called out of the kindness of her heart and he'd made her feel foolish and desperate.

Just like ten years ago.

"This is who he is, Miriam," she told herself as

she poured more wine. "A man who owns a sixteen-million-dollar mansion he rarely visits. A man whose only interest is to increase his bank statement and buy up beautiful bits of land because he can."

She swallowed a mouthful of wine and considered that, as much disdain as she'd had for Chase's mother then and still, Eleanor Ferguson had been right.

Miriam and Chase were better off apart.

Four

Miriam hadn't been in her mother's kitchen for more than five minutes before she started airing her grievances about Chase and the phone call from last night.

Kristine was placing freshly baked rolls into a basket and her brother Ross snatched another one and dunked the end of it into the gravy.

"He's the mayor of what?" their older brother asked around a bite.

"Dallas, dummy," Kris replied. "And stop eating my rolls. I made three dozen and you've already snarfed three of them."

"Four." He argued. His mouth curling into a Grinchy smile.

Kristine sacrificed one more that she tossed at him, but Ross, former college football player that he was, caught it easily, struck a Heisman pose and absconded to the dining room.

"He doesn't act thirty-nine," Kris grumbled. "Anyway. Chase is a jerk and I'm sorry you had to deal with that."

"Yeah, well. I'm sorry I didn't say what I thought to say until *after* I hung up."

"Such as." Kristine motioned with a roll for Miriam to go on.

"I would've informed him that I wasn't one of his underlings and I deserved better treatment than a haughty *No. Thank you*." She dipped her voice into a dopey tone that didn't sound like him, but made her feel better. "I'd have told him that I became a success without his billions and in a field where I wasn't causing global warming. My line of work is admirable."

"It is, sweetie."

"Thank you."

Miriam had completed her degree in agricultural sciences, going on to do compliance work behind a desk for a few years until she realized how wholly unsatisfying it was to push papers from one side of her desk to another. Five years ago, she'd found the Montana Conservation Society and stumbled into her calling. She'd started as program manager and was then promoted to director of student affairs. She mostly worked with teenagers. She taught them how to respect their environment and care for the world they all shared. She found it incredibly rewarding to watch those kids grow and change. Several of the students who came through MCS wouldn't so much as step on an ant if they could help it by the time she was through with them.

And yet Chase had dismissed her like she was a temp on his payroll.

"I should've gone over to his big, audacious house and told him what I think of his wasteful habits and egomaniacal behavior."

"Who, dear?" Her mother stepped into the kitchen and gestured to the basket of rolls. "Kristine, to the table with those, please. We're about to start."

"No one," Miriam answered. "Just… No one."

Kris shuffled into the dining room and Judy Andrix watched her go before narrowing her eyes and squaring her jaw. Since Miriam's father, Alan, had died five years ago of complications from heart surgery, her mom had taken it on herself to play both the role of mom and dad. It wasn't easy for any of them to lose him, but their mother had taken the brunt of that blow. Thirty-nine years of marriage was a lifetime.

"Miriam, would you grab those bottles of wine and take them to the table for me?"

"Sure thing." Relieved the conversation was over, she did as she was asked.

Halfway into dinner, however, her wine remained untouched and her food mostly uneaten.

"Meems, what's going on in your world?" Wendy's girlfriend, Rosalie, asked conversationally.

Miriam blinked out of her stupor and realized she'd been staring at her mashed potatoes, Chase on her mind. "Work. That's about it."

"How did the camp go this summer? I meant to ask but I was so busy."

Busy being a surgeon. It happened.

Miriam filled her in on the camp for eighth graders she'd cochaperoned. "You haven't lived until you've been in charge of thirty hormone-riddled teens in tents."

Wendy nudged Rosalie with her shoulder. "That's what I keep warning her about every time she brings up having children."

"Children are great," Ross's wife, Cecilia, said at the exact moment their five-year-old daughter Raven threw her butter-covered roll on the floor.

"Raven!" While Ross went about explaining to his daughter that the food belonged on her plate and not on the rug, Wendy and Rosalie answered questions from Kristine about having children. Surrogate, they agreed, but they weren't against adoption.

Mom interjected that she didn't care *how* any of them went about it so long as she was given another grandchild.

"Or two," she added with a pointed look at Kris and Brendan, who wisely filled his mouth full of stuffing rather than comment. "Meems, have you been seeing anyone?"

And that's when the last strand on the rope of Miriam's dwindling patience snapped.

"I'm sorry." She stood abruptly from the table and the room silenced. Even Raven seemed to sense the importance of the moment and stopped her complaining. Every pair of eyes swiveled to Miriam. "I have to run an errand."

"What? Now?" Her mother's voice rose.

"I'll be back in an hour, tops. That leaves plenty of time for dessert. Feel free to start playing games without me." She could easily make the round trip to Bigfork and back before the traditional board game battle began. And she didn't mind at all ousting herself from a conversation involving families and children when there was a man very nearby who was going about his evening as if she didn't matter. Been there, done that. She didn't care to suffer a repeat of ten years ago.

Miriam rushed into the kitchen and rifled through her mother's cupboard for a plastic storage container. She sliced one of her pies and slid three large wedges into the container before snapping on the lid. She'd show him what he was missing all right.

She was pulling her coat over her shoulders when her mother appeared in the doorway of the kitchen. Judy eyed the pie in the container.

"Where on earth are you going in the middle of Thanksgiving dinner?" Her mother was a narrow, thin woman whose supermodel good looks couldn't be ignored, even if she was in her early sixties.

"I don't expect you to understand." Miriam gave her mother's arm a squeeze. "But there's someone I *have* to talk to or I won't be able to enjoy a single second of my holiday. I just… It's something I have to do."

"And a phone call won't cut it?" Judy leveled a knowing smile at her third child.

"No." Miriam wouldn't risk a repeat of that robotic blowoff from last night.

"It's snowing again."

It was, but… "I have four-wheel drive."

"I suppose if I stand here and try to talk you out of it, you'll go anyway, only a little later than you intended on account of my keeping you." Her mother folded her arms over her chest. She knew her daughter well.

"One hour. Tops." Miriam repeated, wrapping her hand around the doorknob.

"At least take the mayor a plate of food," her mother called before Miriam could escape. "You can't *only* show up with pie."

"How did you—?" Miriam leaned around her mother to glare beyond the doorway where Kristine sat in Dad's former seat at the table.

Kris blew a kiss and waggled her fingers in a wave.

Only a year old, the Ford F-150 was equipped to glide through snow like it was popped corn. But as she drove closer to Bigfork, the visibility dropped and it was more like trudging through wet sand. It wasn't "her" truck, per se, but had been provided graciously by MCS. She'd been begging for two years for a vehicle that could haul, tow and not give out if she had to drive up a mountain and rescue someone's lost dog. Sure, that had only happened *once*, but she'd had to hike most of it on foot since her compact car hadn't been equipped for the elements. It was practical for her to have a vehicle that could handle Montana's terrain.

Thanks to those elements, the twenty-minute drive to Bigfork was stretching to sixty. She'd encountered traffic and low visibility, and on top of that her gas gauge was dangerously close to E. At a top speed of twelve miles per hour, she was getting nowhere *slowly*. Because she'd underestimated the weatherman and overestimated her F-150, there was no way she'd make it back to her mother's house in this mess.

But Miriam still intended to make her way to Chase's. She wasn't giving up a scant few miles from his house. No way.

At a stoplight, she keyed in a quick text to Kris. I'm going to be celebrating at home alone tonight! Bigfork is buried. :(

Before the stoplight turned green, Miriam's phone rang.

"You have to come back!" Kris said in greeting.

"It's a mess out here." Windshield wipers swiped away the gathering snow and Miriam turned right toward Pinecone Drive and the mayor of Dallas.

"I thought that storm was supposed to miss us."

"Yeah, well, evidently Bigfork caught the edge of it. I'm in a winter wonderland."

"You're still on the road?" asked her downtrodden sister.

"I am, but I'm almost home. Tell everyone I'm sorry. I'll call later when I get settled." She forced a smile as she mentally kicked her own butt for leaving her mom's house. "Hey, maybe you can video chat me in later."

"Is that Miriam? Is she all right?" their mother called in the distance.

"She's fine!" Kris called back. Then to Miriam, "I'll let her know you're all right and home safe… That is where you're going, right? Home?"

"Of course."

"Meems."

"I have to go." Miriam hung up on Kris, who clearly could not be trusted with sensitive information, and resumed her drive to Chase's mansion. If Miriam didn't go to him like she'd vowed, the entire trip would be a waste.

Once she looked him in the eye and made sure he understood who she'd become, she could be on her way. Who was she? A woman who didn't take crap from anyone. A woman who'd found herself *and* her way in the decade that separated them. Her biggest worry was that she'd remained a still frame in his mind: standing next to a private plane, tears running down her face, begging him not to leave.

Or worse, the one who'd emailed and called him after she'd come home to Montana. She'd been so weak back then, but Chase had always maintained his strength.

"Clean break," he'd told her, and he'd meant it.

Meanwhile, she'd continued to declare her love for him and had reiterated her claim that they were meant to be. Never had she been so wrong before or since.

Chase's mother, Eleanor, had seen Miriam not as a lifelong mate for her son, but a preoccupation he couldn't afford. Miriam knew because the only phone call answered from Chase's cell phone happened to be answered by Eleanor herself.

On Thanksgiving.

Miriam blinked in shock. She'd completely forgotten that fact.

But yes, it'd been Thanksgiving. She remembered excusing herself from the room while her siblings and parents were unboxing a new board game. Then she'd shut herself in Kristine's bedroom and called Chase. She'd been thinking then about how she was the only one of them at the table not coupled off.

The more things changed...

She heard those words in her late father's voice, her heart squeezing as she remembered his big laugh and bigger presence. He'd been comforting, but notably frustrated while she nursed her broken heart that winter. He'd been exactly what a father should be.

She turned into the lakeside neighborhood where the wealthiest residents of Bigfork lived, rolled by the snowy, pricey new builds with their lack of trees and yard space, and toward the older part of the neighborhood. The houses closer to the lake sat on high hills, were spread much farther apart and had exponentially higher price tags.

Ten minutes of slow-crawling her way toward Pinecone Drive, and she was navigating through dark trees and an abandoned road piled deep with snow.

This is a bad idea.

Not braving the storm—she was confident in her driving abilities and her trusty Ford to get her both in *and* out of this mess—but confronting Chase. That phone call from ten years ago replayed in her mind and her gloved hands gripped the steering wheel, her shoulders wilting.

Chase Ferguson's phone. Who is this?

The woman who'd answered had been older. An air of sophistication outlined every word she spoke. Miriam had recognized Eleanor's voice instantly, but she refused to let the woman bully her. Her future with Chase involved only them—or so she'd believed.

Listen, darling. I appreciate that you have an affinity for my son, however I can't allow this to continue. He has aspirations for a political seat. He has a future involving Ferguson Oil. Can you honestly tell me that you wouldn't be a hindrance to those goals? If you love him, truly, you'll support him by letting him live his life here in Dallas without you.

Miriam never found out if Chase had asked his

mother to handle his dirty work for him, or if Eleanor had taken the call and kept her son in the dark. In the end, Miriam guessed it didn't matter.

She'd reached out. He'd stayed hidden.

Dumb. Dumb of her to come tonight.

At the base of the gargantuan property, she waited for the wipers to swipe the gathering snow from the windshield to assess the situation. The property was nestled in the trees, the clearing blocked by a gate with a keypad she'd have to drive up to. Her truck would make it, of that she was sure. And even if she wasn't, she wasn't risking using the last of her fuel to turn back. She could only hope that Chase had a few gallons of gasoline to fill her tank up so that she could drive home, or else…

No. She wasn't entertaining that thought.

She climbed the steep, snowy hill, her tires sliding enough that her heart hammered against her throat. Thankfully, the driveway evened out at the gate so she didn't slide backwards in the snow. She pressed a button on a callbox to request to be let in. A camera lens attached to the device stared at her from its unblinking mechanical eye. Miriam grabbed the container of sweet potato pie from the passenger seat.

While she waited, snow covered her windshield and drifted inside. *He might not be here*, she thought miserably. Or maybe he'd been caught in the storm while gathering supplies and was holed up in a hotel somewhere—

"Mimi." Chase's low timbre sailed out of the speaker, at once surprised and scolding.

"Hi." She waggled the container. "Pie delivery. I won't stay long." There was a significant pause, but no response. She swore she could feel his laser-like glare through the camera. A buzz sounded as the iron gates swung aside through the gathering snow.

The white stuff on the driveway was untouched by tires or boot prints. After debating leaving her truck running, she shut it off to save fuel and climbed out. The walkway to the front door had been shoveled at some point, but since then a few inches of snow had filled in the gaps.

She shuddered as icy wind sliced through her hair, the temperature colder coming off the frigid lake below. A porch light snapped on and Chase appeared outside wearing a sweater and jeans and sneakers that didn't appear weather resistant.

"Running shoes in this weather. Are you crazy?" She pulled three containers filled with his dinner and dessert from the passenger seat and then shut the door.

"You're calling me crazy? What the hell are you doing here?"

"I told you I won't be long." She shoved the pie container into his hand and his scowl deepened. Her teeth chattered, partially from nerves. This was the moment she'd been waiting for—to set Chase Ferguson straight. On her terms. She glanced around at the pale moonlit mounds of snow. Okay, not exactly her terms, but it was too late to back out now.

"Get inside," he commanded, his breath visible in the cold. Out of habit she locked her truck and it beeped briefly, letting her know. Chase glared over her shoulder at the sound, but she refused to let him scare her off from what she came here to say. She was going to set him straight, then turn this big bastard around and drive straight home.

Do not pass Go. Do not collect $200.

She'd really miss playing games with her family tonight. A dart of regret shocked her ribcage. And then a dart of something else when Chase cupped her elbow and started toward the house.

"Watch your step," his low voice rumbled as he gestured to the nearly invisible porch steps. "You'd better have a good reason for being here other than bringing me pie."

Oh, no worries, Mayor McCheese. I have one.

Five

Chase had known Miriam was headstrong, but driving through a snowstorm to bring him dinner was a touch more than headstrong. It was dangerous. Miriam being in danger wasn't acceptable—especially when he was the cause.

Inside, he shut the door behind them as she checked out the interior of the house. He looked with her, admiring the rich warm-colored woods and the tall, beamed ceilings. Every inch of this place had been polished to dustless perfection, and it should've been, given what he paid his housekeepers.

Logs were stacked in the fireplace, the matches sitting next to a newspaper pages he'd twisted for kindling. He'd left his task when the buzzer to the gate rang. He'd had groceries for the week delivered that morning and a cord of firewood had been delivered after that. The weatherman had predicted the storm with its massive amounts of snow to miss Bigfork, but Chase wasn't taking the risk. Luckily, he'd heeded the warnings and overprepared…which was less than he could say for his gorgeous houseguest.

"Would you mind directing me to the 'wing' where you keep your kitchen, Daddy Warbucks?" Mimi asked with a snide smile.

Nice to see her sharp wit was intact.

"What are you doing here?" It was the most obvious question and the answer she should have offered upon showing up unannounced at his doorstep.

"You said if I needed anything…" She craned her chin to look up at him since he'd already ascended the three steps leading to the kitchen. She was even more beautiful than he remembered. Her cheeks had lost some of their fullness allowing rose-colored cheekbones to angle across her model-like features. The thinness of her face made her lips appear even more plump—and far more kissable than they ought to.

He took the remaining containers from her and gestured to the entryway closet with his head. "Hang up your coat."

"I'm not staying that long. The storm is worsening and—"

"And you're going to wait it out here." Over his dead body she'd navigate through this blizzard tonight.

"No. I will not be doing that." Her eyebrows climbed her forehead. "But I will accept a gallon or two of gas for the short drive home from here. I don't want to get—"

"Coat, Mimi." He came down the stairs to hover

over her, his nostrils flared. "Then walk past the living room, take a right and you'll see the kitchen."

"I'll follow you," she snapped, but slipped her coat off and draped it over her arm.

He could do without the attitude, but at least she'd met him halfway.

He settled the containers—one with the sweet potato pie she'd showed him at the gate and the other two overflowing with Thanksgiving dinner.

A long *would you get a load of this* whistle of appreciation came from behind him.

"Wow. Every inch of this place is more amazing than the last."

She turned a one-eighty as she inventoried the kitchen: the wide island in the center, the floor-to-ceiling cabinets, six-burner gas stove, and a shiny, double-doored fridge. She tossed her coat over one of the stools at the island. Slim jeans accentuated her mile-long legs and a cranberry sweater with a scoop neck revealed creamy, pale skin. No cleavage—a fact she'd bemoaned plenty when they were together a decade ago. He couldn't have cared less. The sight of her in a string bikini, and the way the chilly lake water caused her nipples to point from behind the bright blue top, had been more than enough to pique his interest.

"Yeah, so turkey, stuffing, green beans. All the basics." She folded her fingers together while she talked. "Sweet potato pie is for dessert, though, I suppose you're grown-up and could spoil your dinner if you wanted. Did you eat?"

"What the hell are you doing here, Mimi?" he repeated.

At his tone, she narrowed eyes as brown as the forest floor. Deep mulch in color and blasting him with an accusation she hadn't spoken yet.

"I'm here—" she pointed at the ground, seeming to gather her courage "—to show you that I'm no longer the besotted twenty-three-year-old you left on an airfield in Dallas. You may be a billionaire oil tycoon politician with a mansion the size of your hometown, but I became someone, too."

"Is that so?" He came out from behind the island in the center of the kitchen and Mimi took a hesitant step back. He wouldn't allow her to make him out to be some billionaire asshole without an argument in his own defense. "Tell me, then, how you're the next incarnation of Mother Teresa."

She snapped her mouth shut then opened it to let out a little tut of surprise. "I didn't say I was Mother Teresa."

"No, but you implied I'm the devil incarnate, so I assumed…"

"You have no idea what I implied. You don't know me. You *knew* me."

"Likewise." He scanned her from chestnut hair to the toes of her knee-high boots. She dressed differently than she used to and not just because the season had changed. There was something more formal about her. Less playful than he remembered. "You grew up. I grew up. It happens."

"Unlike you, I don't sit around counting the zeroes in my bank account. I actually *help* people."

"So do I. Are you going to cut the crap and tell me why you're here?" It was the last time he was going to ask.

"I just did! You weren't listening on the phone, so I had to come here in person to—"

"Bullshit. You made a twenty-minute drive—"

"That took over an hour."

"—in this weather carting cold Thanksgiving dinner and my favorite pie. Don't tell me you came all this way to put me in my place."

Her pink tongue touched lips painted cranberry red to match her sweater. He knew too well that unlike the tart fruit, she tasted as sweet as honey.

"I thought you'd appreciate it."

"I do. But that doesn't explain why you're here."

She shrugged with one dark eyebrow and tightened plush lips he'd kissed more times than he could recall. He'd made every attempt to kiss the sunshine off her skin that summer. Back then he could've buried his nose in her coconut-scented hair and never come up for air.

Until reality had intruded.

"I tried to invite you to dinner at my family's house so you wouldn't have to eat alone," she huffed.

"So I'm the equivalent of a stray dog in need of a bone." He spread his arms to indicate the expansive room in which he was standing. "Do I look like I can't fend for myself?"

"You said no!" she practically shouted.

"As was my prerogative."

What was she up to? He kept his voice even, his tone neutral. He'd been yelled at by a great number of people in his career, and it was his second nature to tamp down any emotions that didn't lead to an effective solution.

The line of her mouth softened. Her eyebrows lowered. Naked vulnerability bled into her expression.

Then he figured it out. It slapped him upside the head, jarring his brain.

I'm an idiot.

"I hurt your feelings," he stated. Could he have been more obtuse? "That's why you're here."

She made a *pfft* sound but he was right. He could tell by the way she shifted her weight onto one boot—almost squirming in his presence. Some things about Mimi had changed in the last ten years, but some things hadn't. She was the same stubborn, beautiful, hopeful woman he'd made love to back then, but with an even sturdier backbone and harder head. She brought him Thanksgiving dinner tonight not because he was a charity case but because—

"It bothered you to picture me eating alone," he told her.

"Why would I care about a pompous, overblown—"

"Admit it."

He heard a deep sucking sound as she pulled in a lungful of oxygen.

"Fine," she blew out on an exhale. "I was sitting in front of a dressed turkey thinking that if you *weren't* such a stubborn jackass, you would've been there enjoying the spoils of a home-cooked meal. Rare in your case, as I recall."

It was true. Eleanor Ferguson didn't cook. She catered.

"I took it upon myself to deliver both dinner and a message, planning to turn and drive straight back to my family's house knowing that you were both fed *and* informed." A crease appeared between her brows.

"Only now I'll be heading to my apartment instead of back for dessert with my family."

He could see and feel the regret coming off her. The expression didn't erase the elegance of her features, and accentuated the firmer, straighter line of her backbone. She was a confusing whirlwind of attributes, but Chase saw through her air of confidence. She couldn't hide behind the one quality she'd never possessed: ambivalence.

Mimi had never been ambivalent or calloused to the needs of others. No matter how badly they'd treated her in the past.

"Tell me more about what you do," he said, turning to lift the lids of the containers.

"What I do?"

"Yes." Even cool, the food was an inviting array of holiday fragrances. Thyme and sage and butter.

"Um. Okay. I'm the director of student affairs for the Montana Conservation Society. I work mostly with teenagers, but I've also spearheaded a recent and very important recycling campaign with a local apartment complex."

He punched the buttons on the microwave—first removing a small plastic container of cranberry sauce thoughtfully included "on the side."

"One of many," Mimi added.

"You're as passionate as I remember." He pulled two forks from a drawer and laid them on the island.

"Is that a nice way of saying I'm misguided?"

"Not at all. The world needs more advocates like you."

Her mouth was frozen in a half gape, like she was shocked he'd paid her a compliment. "Thank you."

"You're welcome."

They stood on opposite sides of the island—what a metaphor for how they'd left things—in silence as the remainder of the seconds ticked down on the microwave before it beeped. He set the containers between him and Mimi, grabbed an open bottle of wine and two glasses and poured himself one.

She placed a finger on the neck of the bottle when he tipped it toward her glass. "I'm leaving."

"I can't let you do that." He poured the wine anyway and set the glass in front of her. She frowned. He offered her a fork. She shook her head.

"I ate already. This is for you."

Chase locked eyes with the woman who used to love him, with the woman he'd nearly loved more than his own common sense. "Thank you."

He dug in, scooping a bite of turkey, mashed potatoes and stuffing, dunking the fork into the cranberry sauce before closing his eyes and savoring the flavors of a slow-cooked, took-all-day-to-make meal. Before he meant to, he moaned his approval.

Without another glance in her direction, he unapologetically took another big bite.

Six

Watching Chase eat bordered on pornographic.

Or maybe Miriam didn't get out much. She rested her top teeth on her bottom lip and watched as he moaned around another bite. Her mouth watered, not for the food, but for *him*. Hearing those familiar moans reminded her of the time they'd spent together. Naked. No holds barred.

Not why you came here, she reminded herself sternly.

Yet here she stood, a woman who'd been literally naked before him, and was at this moment metaphorically naked before him. He'd figured out—before she'd admitted it to herself—that she'd come here not only to give him a piece of her mind but also to give herself the comfort of knowing he'd had a home-cooked meal on Thanksgiving.

With one masculine hand, he cradled the red wine, swirled the liquid in the glass and took a sip. She watched his throat work while he swallowed, her own going dry. It was an erotic scene to take in for a woman who was currently not having sex with anyone but herself.

She balled her fist as a flutter of desire took flight between her thighs. Now she wanted wine, dammit. And maybe to touch him. Just once.

He heartily ate another scoop of his food, then pushed her wine glass closer to her. An offer.

An offer she wouldn't accept.

Couldn't accept.

She wasn't unlike Little Red Riding Hood, having run to the wrong house for shelter. Only in this case, the Big Bad Wolf wasn't dining on Red's beloved grandmother but Miriam's family's home cooking.

An insistent niggling warned her that she could be next—and hadn't this particular "wolf" already consumed her heart?

"So, I'm going to go." She'd risk her gas tank running dry before she stayed another minute and found herself trapped with him.

When she grabbed her coat and stood, a warm hand grasped her much cooler one. Chase's fingers stroked hers before lightly squeezing, his eyes studying her for a long moment, his fork hovering over his unfinished dinner.

Finally, he said, "I'll see you out."

"That's not necessary."

He did as he pleased and stood, his hand on her lower back as he walked with her. Outside, the wind pushed against the front door, causing the wood to creak. She and Chase exchanged glances. Had she waited too long?

"For the record, I don't want you to leave."

What she'd have given to hear those words on that airfield ten years ago.

"I'll be all right."

"You can't know that." He frowned out of either concern or anger, she couldn't tell which. "How was the hill?"

She shrugged one shoulder and wouldn't look him in the eye. His sloped driveway had been slick, but she'd made it... Barely. She wasn't looking forward to going back down.

"Mimi—" His phone rang and he reached into his pocket. Whatever he'd been about to say to her hung in the air like the sexual tension that was once between them. It wasn't here now, but *something* was. If she were being honest, she might describe it as sadness. Or hope. Funny how hard those two were to tell apart.

Chase's side of the conversation was filled with one- or two-word responses giving her no idea who he was talking to or what about. "I see. Thank you. Yes." Until the farewell. "You too, Emmett."

"Emmett?" She knew that name... She narrowed her eyes, her mind seeking the particular storage cabinet for that nugget of information while Chase pocketed his phone. A second later she located the memory. "Your friend, Emmett? The one who had several torrid affairs here in Bigfork while you..."

She trailed off. *While you just had the one with me.*

Chase hadn't been interested in multiple girls that summer. Remarkably, amidst a beach littered with tiny bikinis stuffed with big breasts and curvy hips,

Miriam had caught his eye. With her plain brown hair and superslim physique, she hadn't expected the tall, dark-haired, muscular specimen playing flip cup with his friends to notice her.

She and her friend Mandie had stood on the sidelines watching as, round after round, his side of the table won each game. He and Emmett would high-five and Chase would smile, all white teeth and tanned skin... She'd fallen in love the moment his eyes clashed with hers, but she'd never dreamed she'd get any nearer to him than the other side of that patch of sand.

"Yes, one and the same." Chase interrupted the memory. The bright colorful summer vision receded into the neutrals of the mansion's interior. His careful smile was a ghost of what it had been and hers was now much harder to earn.

"I'm glad you're still friends." She'd long ago lost touch with Mandie, her work friend when she'd been waiting tables at the Crab Shucker that summer. She hadn't thought of Mandie in ages, but now Miriam wondered what became of her. Mandie had gone home with Emmett back then. Neither of them had any interest in a second night together, despite Mandie's raving that he was *the lay of the year*. She advised Miriam not to get *too caught up on that Texas boy*, meaning Chase, but Miriam had been completely caught up.

So, Eleanor Ferguson wasn't the only one right about their relationship. Maybe it really had been in Miriam's head—the love she'd been so sure she felt for him. Maybe it'd been mere appreciation. Infatuation...

"Stay." Chase's gray-green eyes were warm and inviting, his voice a time capsule back to not-soinnocent days. The request was siren-call sweet, but she'd not risk herself for it.

"No." She yanked open the front door, shocked when the howling wind shoved her back a few inches. Snow billowed in, swirling around her feet, and her now wet, cold fingers slipped from the knob.

Chase caught her, an arm looped around her back, and shoved the door closed with the flat of one palm. She hung there, suspended by the corded forearm at her back, clutching his shirt in one fist, and nearly drowned in his lake-colored eyes.

"I can stay for a while longer," she squeaked, the decision having been made for her.

His handsome face split into a brilliant smile and a laugh bobbed his throat. He released her and moved away, robbing her of his heat and attention. She hated how cold she felt with him gone. It was like a cloud had come out to mask the sun.

"Melodramatic much?" she mumbled to herself, hanging her coat in the entryway closet. Then she followed where he went. That, too, was a reaction she wasn't going to explore.

He stood in the center of the sunken living room and flipped on the television over the hearth. A local station was sharing the latest weather report from Bigfork. A windblown, red-faced woman confirmed Miriam's fears.

"Travel of any sort is not only dangerous but could be life-threatening!" Gale Schneider, broadcasting from what appeared to be the inside of a violently shaken snow globe, shouted over the wind. The hood of her downy coat was up, but the wind lashed, blowing the material like a flag on a pole. "Montana authorities warn that anyone watching should stay where they are unless they absolutely must travel!" she continued. "If you're in your vehicle, you may want to find the closest open service station or convenience store until the storm blows over. Back to you, Joan."

A little spike of fear stabbed her belly.

"Mother Nature and your local weather reporter agree with me," Chase told her. He pointed the remote and the television winked off. "You're staying. No sense in risking driving home to your empty apartment."

She hated that she agreed with him.

"Is there anything you need from your truck that might make your stay here more comfortable?" His voice was seductive and low, the offer sincere and chivalrous.

"My purse," she confirmed numbly. "And my overnight bag." She'd never taken it into her mother's house since her arms were full of pie and she'd been put to work the moment she crossed the kitchen's threshold.

"That's convenient." His eyebrows jumped and he walked past her. She warred with the urge to explain herself, but decided against it. She'd come in here with her defenses up and where had that landed her?

She regretted having been robbed of her grand exit. After declaring what a successful adult she'd become, she really, *really* wanted to watch Chase's mansion dwindle in the rearview mirror. It would have been poetic.

From the entryway closet where he was pulling on his coat, he said, "I'll need your keys."

"Sure you can handle the snow, Dallas?" she asked

on her approach. "I can. I'm a born-and-bred Montanan."

"And I'm a born-and-bred Texan. I'm not afraid of a little snow." He popped the collar on his coat and held out his palm. She dropped her keyring into it.

Before he slipped out the door, he said, "Don't eat my pie."

After reassuring her entire family she was fine—*really, yes, really, I'm fine, stop asking*—Miriam pressed the end button on her cell and stared out the window at the whitewashed landscape.

From her vantage point in the sunken living room, she couldn't see farther than the deck. She knew what was down there—the lake and a good portion of the shoreline that Chase owned along with this property. In another life, she'd been bikini clad on that beach, making out with the man she was snowed in with tonight.

Life had a twisted sense of humor.

Kristine's reaction had bordered on comical once she'd learned that Miriam was in Chase's mansion. She'd darted to another part of their mother's house and hissed into the phone, "Do not have sex with him!"

"Only if you swear to keep it a secret that I'm here," Miriam volleyed back.

Kris had humbly apologized for letting the mayor out of the bag, but she wasn't through yet. "Do *not* have sex with that disgustingly beautiful man, Meems. Remember, this is not a second chance. You're not trapped with him because fate said so, but because you're too stubborn not to drive into a snowstorm to deliver the man pie."

Miriam had lowered her voice—though there was no need, since Chase was in the kitchen, which was approximately the width of her entire apartment's floor plan—and assured her sister that it'd be a cold day in hell before that happened.

She was acutely aware it was a cold day indeed and further aware that this might be hell since she was stranded with the former object of her passion and affection.

Again with the melodrama?

She'd told herself repeatedly that she'd leave the moment the snow stopped, but she'd also been watching Gale on TV, and even on Mute, Miriam's plan was becoming the stuff of fiction.

"Do you at least have condoms?" Kris had asked.

At which point, Miriam said goodbye and ended the call. Why would she have condoms? She'd planned on attending a family weekend as a happy single, not getting naked with the mayor of Dallas.

That…shouldn't sound as inviting as it did.

The snow swirled outside the wide windows and her vision blurred at the edges. She really was stuck here.

"Last chance." A velvet voice smoothed over her shoulder.

She blinked the winter wonderland into focus and turned to find an offered plate with a single slice of sweet potato pie in the middle.

Chase held up a shiny, tined instrument. "I brought you a clean fork."

"Did you like it?" She inhaled, catching some of his sandalwood-and-spice smell in her nostrils.

"Exquisite."

What a Chase Ferguson word. He'd always had a formal edge alongside the rough-and-tumble. Then she'd met his parents and figured out why. He was practically royalty—not that they had royalty in the United States but she imagined billionaires as their *own* sort of royalty.

"If you liked it so much, why offer me your last piece?"

"The gentlemanly thing to do would've been to offer you the *first* piece, Mimi. Who the hell have you been dating for the last ten years?"

"You don't want to know," she said around a low chuckle. For a split second—maybe even half a second—she understood why her sister warned her against falling into bed with him again. Damn, he was charming.

"Share it with you?" She accepted the fork, noticing his fork pressed into his other palm.

"I was hoping you'd say that." Just like that, they were coexisting in a moment of amicability.

"Let's sit." He took his seat in the middle of the plush walnut-colored leather sofa, forcing her to take the seat next to him. Her leg brushed his and warmth seeped through her jeans.

She ignored the nervous skip of her heart and ate a forkful of pie. "Not bad for my first time."

"You nailed it," he told her, taking a bite himself.

"Why are you here in Bigfork?"

He finished chewing before answering. And when he did, he leaned a hairbreadth closer to her.

"I suppose you're looking for a bigger answer than vacation."

She let her silence be her "Yes."

"It was already scheduled when your photo crossed my desk. If that article goes live and the press finds out I'm in the same city as you, it'll be a circus."

"But you didn't reschedule your trip."

He ate another bite of pie. "I don't make decisions based on what might happen."

Didn't she know that too well? He hadn't taken the chance on her based on "what might happen" either.

Her gaze snagged on her suitcase standing in the mouth of the hallway.

"I guess this situation would look bad."

"Not bad." He offered her the plate holding the last bite. "But definitely…conspicuous. I don't have anything to hide from the press. Do you?"

Seven

Short of sitting in a tree at Mountainway Park to keep it from being chopped down, or driving ten miles over the speed limit, or skinny-dipping with Chase in Flathead Lake, Miriam didn't make a habit of breaking the law. She imagined he would've disagreed with saving a tree that she'd later learned was infested with ash borer beetles, but he'd give her a pass when it came to the speeding. And she knew exactly how he'd felt about stripping naked and cannonballing into Flathead Lake off a private dock—firmly *against*. But once she'd goaded him properly, he'd stripped down and dived in, resurfacing in the moonlight wearing a huge smile a few seconds later.

They hadn't agreed on everything, and she'd argued her differing points of view fervently while they were together. He had nothing against the oil industry—

later, she'd learned why—but they'd always agreed to disagree and then made out, their lips fusing and disqualifying their brains from further participation. Arguments made up a small part of their summer together. Mostly, they'd made love and stared into each other's eyes, hardly able to believe they'd found their other half...

Or at least *she'd* done that.

"You know, I will have some wine." She burst off the sofa and moved to the kitchen. A scant glass of red would be enough to calm her, but wouldn't erase the recurring memories. Evidently nothing would keep them at bay. She splashed a few more inches into the glass he'd left on the kitchen island for her and swallowed a drink.

He joined her, placing the empty pie plate in the sink and palming his own balloon-shaped glass.

"What would you have been doing this evening if you weren't trapped here with me?"

"'Trapped' is an interesting way to phrase it." The next sip tasted better than the last. "My brother and two sisters and their significant others are most likely embroiled in a board-game battle. We save Monopoly for last since it's better to play when everyone's had more wine."

"Ah, Monopoly. Ender of relationships."

She couldn't picture Chase doing something as commonplace as playing board games. Unless it was backgammon. Chess, maybe. Whatever games stuffy rich people played.

She frowned at the unkind thought, but then gave herself a pass. She hadn't seen him in ten years, so it was wholly possible he *was* the Monopoly guy—

minus the monocle—gobbling up property to expand his portfolio. Making under-the-table deals with dirty politicians to advance his own gain. Sweeping the Free Parking money and hiding his spoils under the board...

"So. What have you been up to since I saw you last?" She sat on one of the stools, resting an elbow on the surface of the island.

Rather than sit, he flattened both hands on the countertop and studied her before answering.

"I was a city council member for a while. Served on the board of public works. Even did a stint at Ferguson Oil as director of something-or-other." He hoisted one eyebrow. "Ruining the environment and all that."

"The oil business is no better for the planet than the cattle business, Chase. You know that."

"What would you have my family do, Miriam? Go into the vegan faux-meat business and start from scratch?"

She felt her cheeks redden in challenge. Determined not to slip into shallow arguments as they had in the past—there'd be no making up by making out tonight—she gestured to the wine bottle. "This is very good. A favorite of yours?"

"One of the favorites. I packed a dozen bottles from my wine cellar and brought them up."

"On your private jet?" She snorted.

"Yes. But I bought a car when I landed," he said, completely serious.

"A problem easily solved for you."

"You didn't used to resent my financial status," he shot back.

Her face was aflame. He was right. She hadn't had

a problem with his financial status back then. Why would she have? He'd been hers. She was too busy building castles in the sky to judge him for being wealthy.

She hid her rosy cheeks behind the wide rim of her wineglass and took another sip, then spoke without looking at him. "I'm sorry. That was rude."

"Tell me more about what you do," he said, smoothly changing the subject. He stood from his lean on the island and reclaimed his wineglass, hip against the far counter instead.

"I work outside a lot. Mostly in the warmer months. Winter is spent planning the spring and summer camps for the kids and writing the itineraries. Though I also help out the wildlife preserve."

"Saving the world."

"What's wrong with saving the world?" she snapped.

"Nothing." His confused frown was sincere. "You should try to save the world, or at least part of it. It's what I'm doing."

Choosing to say nothing seemed the best response. She pressed her lips together.

"I crowd them out," he continued explaining. "The bad guys. Someone who would take advantage of the city funds and allow his or her palm to be greased by those who want special treatment. If I'm in office, those guys aren't."

She'd never thought of it that way.

"Last year my sister Stefanie helped me organize a fund-raiser for adoptions for families who couldn't conceive." He tilted his head, a teasing spark in his eye. "Or can you also find something wrong with my supporting orphans, too?"

No, she really couldn't. And that was the problem. She couldn't vilify him, which meant liking him again. And liking him could lead to...

Nothing.

She would never allow her liking him to lead to anything more. The risk was too great.

"Look, we don't have to make peace with what happened between us, Mimi," he said, reading her mind, "but we do have to live together for an evening. Can we table the discussions revolving around the topics we argue about? Focus on the ones we agree upon?"

"Is there one?" She finished her wine and sent a longing look at the bottle, wrestling with the idea of sinking into the reprieve of a second glass.

"We agree on two topics so far. Pie. And wine." He tipped the bottle over her glass and poured. She admired his strong fingers and tanned skin. How could a man's hand be sexy?

Because it's attached to the rest of him.

Right. Good point.

"I'm going to start a fire," he said. "Sit up a while. The bedroom on the top floor is where I'm staying, but feel free to take your pick of the others."

Chase left Miriam to her...whatever was going on with her, and finished stacking the firewood and kindling in the hearth.

She'd vanished down the hallway, declining his offer to carry her suitcase or show her around.

"I assume the bedrooms are the ones with beds," she'd quipped.

Once the fire was crackling, he stayed where he was on the rug, kicked off his sneakers and reached for his wineglass. All the tableau was missing was a sleeping golden retriever sitting by his red-and-white-patterned socks.

Mimi had been gruff and short with him at the same time she'd been kind and hesitant. He could guess she would have preferred to come stomping in here and read him his rights, but she'd never been able to be truly cruel. He wondered if that's how she thought he'd treated her back when they split. *Cruelly.*

Seemed crueler to him at the time to drag her away from her family and the lake town she loved and into a world of politics and oil—both of which she'd hated then and was clearly no fonder of now.

When he'd first spotted her on the video at the gate, he hadn't believed his own eyes. And when she'd climbed from her truck while he stood in the frigid snow watching her advance, he'd made a decision then and there.

She wasn't leaving his house without fully understanding where he'd stood all those years ago. She wasn't the only one with an axe to bury.

He'd lied to her earlier when he said there were two topics they agreed upon. There was a third area where they'd excelled. In bed. Or, on the beach. In the car. He was equally sure they'd be able to navigate that particular act without fail now, and in a variety of locations.

Underneath her need to put him in his place, her high chin and straight shoulders, was the soft, warm woman who'd rested against his side. The giving, loving woman who'd opened up an entirely new world to him. Mimi wasn't a hookup—she never had been.

And maybe that'd been the problem. They'd taken each other seriously in those stolen summer months. And when her roommate was out of town, he'd stayed the weekend, allowing himself to linger in the moments between Mimi's deep, quiet breaths before the sun had come up. He'd stumbled into a rare and precious woman, and had never found a replica.

Yet it'd all been a fantasy. And like all fantasies, destined to end.

When it came time to take her home to Dallas to meet his family, she'd shrunk against him. Dallas wasn't where Mimi belonged. She belonged somewhere surrounded by leaves and streams, not concrete and steel and glass.

By the time she'd met his parents and he'd felt the turgid chill coming off his mother, the fantasy had crumbled to dust. Not only did Mimi not belong in Dallas. She didn't belong *with him*. And he'd have seen that clearly had he met her any time other than during the lakeside summer vacation. His head hadn't been on straight and Mimi… God, Mimi. She'd been lovesick. It'd nearly killed him to do what was right for her and damn his own heart.

But he had.

He was twenty-six at the time and no more able to know who he wanted to spend forever with than what corner of politics he'd end up occupying. Hell, he'd had his sights on president of the United States at one point, an office he knew now he wouldn't hold if he were the last qualified candidate on earth.

A door closing brought him back to the present

before the faint sound of a shower running filled his mind's eye with Mimi's slim frame, lithe legs and pert, round breasts. The first time she'd untied the string on her bikini top and flashed him, he'd stared slack-jawed at her pale skin, lightly freckled from the sun, and known he'd do anything to have her.

He shifted from his cross-legged seat on the rug, his thoughts looping a similar track tonight. To hold that fiery, uncertain, passionate woman against him again would be…

"Wrong," he said aloud.

But as he reminded himself of that, a certain part of him stirred from dormant sleep when he pictured her beneath him. Or on top of him.

"Hell." He pinched the bridge of his nose and blew out a breath. As impossible as it would seem in this circumstance—as great as the chances of his failure were, he wanted her like he'd wanted her the first time he caught sight of her on that crowded beach ten years ago.

He hadn't been able to resist the tantalizing and confusing combination of sensitivity and strength, wrapped in a tangle of poise and chutzpah. Now that he'd gone ten years without meeting a woman who possessed even half of Mimi Andrix's attributes, he'd likely go another ten once their stint in this mansion ended.

And he wasn't the only one who'd noticed the spark between them.

When they were sharing pie, her eyes had lingered on his mouth. He'd wanted to lean forward to sample her lips and damn the consequences, but the timing had been off.

So. He'd make sure her response was favorable before he moved forward.

But yes, he decided. He was definitely moving forward.

Eight

Miriam emerged from the bathroom after her shower, hair dry since she'd washed it yesterday, her striped pajama pants paired with a Montana State University sweatshirt over a T-shirt. She opted for no bra after a bit of hesitation, but who was she kidding? It wasn't as if corralling "the girls" into a brassiere was necessary—not for her.

In stockinged feet, she shuffled out of the bedroom she'd chosen, pleased with her pick. It boasted a queen bed and was large enough for a stuffed chair by the window. A flat-screen television was mounted over the dresser, and had a private bathroom attached. It was as close to a hotel suite as she could come.

She'd climbed under the covers and flipped through TV channels, but nothing kept her mind from wandering beyond her borrowed bedroom door. She was wide awake and hyperaware that there was a man on the other side of the house.

She assumed Chase was still awake. He'd been a night owl like her that summer, but many things had changed since then. Maybe he was no longer nocturnal.

She decided to find out.

She found him sitting on the corner of the sofa, legs crossed at the ankles, frowning down at his phone. He was still dressed in a sweater and jeans, the jaunty design of his socks causing her to smile. *Not so buttoned-up after all.* The way he was lounging in front of a fire he'd built made him appear welcoming. Comfortable.

Maybe that's why she plucked her half-full wineglass from the island and sat on the love seat across from him.

He looked up when she sat, but she kept her eyes on the fire, feeling not the least bit sleepy.

"Get settled?" he asked after a prolonged beat where neither of them spoke.

"Yes. Thank you."

He rested his elbows on his knees and tossed the phone onto a wood-and-metal coffee table that was both modern and rustic.

"Do you stay up late every night or only during snowed-in vacations?" she asked.

"Are you questioning my nocturnal habits?" He let the question hang and she fought the urge to think about sex. Specifically, sex with him.

"I have no right to judge what you do at night," she said. *Or who you do.* There was an unpleasant thought—Chase sharing a bed with another woman.

Not that she had any claim over him, but the thought was still unsavory.

"Yes, whatever you do, don't question my sleepless nights filled with reading biographies or complicated state plans." His lips quirked at one corner, an even split of confidence and self-deprecation. "How about you? You don't appear to miss much beauty sleep."

"I'm not much for early to bed, early to rise," she said, refusing to acknowledge his sideways compliment.

"I'm already healthy, wealthy and wise," he quipped, finishing the saying she'd started. "Why mess with perfection?"

"Oh, so you're perfect now."

"My methods. Not me."

And humble, she thought, keeping her smile hidden. With a subtle shake of her head, she sipped her wine.

"What room did you choose?"

"The smaller one near the kitchen. With the en suite."

"The one with the stone shower?"

"That's the one." Stone walls and a glass partition separated the shower from the rest of the bathroom. No rods or shower curtain rings—just a big open square with a rainfall-style shower overhead. Bliss.

"I showered in there the day I got here."

The idea of sharing a shower with him—well not *sharing*, but kinda—was a distracting thought. She drank a little more wine.

"Seemed a waste to only use the shower upstairs."

"Your room's the largest I take it?" she happily changed the subject.

"It's the largest. Has its own sitting area. Overlooks the trees, the lake. There's a fireplace in the corner. I'll show it to you later."

She would've liked to convince herself that she'd imagined the heat in his eyes at what could be an innocuous invitation, but it was there, all right. Darkening the gray-green to smoky jade and knocking her for a hell of a loop.

"I'd planned on making a fire in there and spending the weekend laid out in the giant bed."

Yes, her cheeks were most definitely aflame at the picture his words evoked. Chase in naught but a pair of low-slung sweats, sheets barely covering his naked torso...

"Now that you're here, hiding out isn't as intriguing."

"Go ahead. I can fend for myself." She cleared her throat and the image from her head. "I know that you have the makings for grilled cheese sandwiches, and a frozen pizza. I'm sure there are eggs in your fridge."

"Right on every count but one. I don't eat eggs."

"Really?" She tried to remember if she'd seen him eating an egg when they dated. "Did you ever?"

"Not really. I mostly eat smoothies with protein powder or toast with avocado slices."

She made a face. "I assume you don't have a box of Froot Loops hiding in your cabinets?"

"Grape-Nuts."

She couldn't help joining him when he laughed.

"It's to go on top of the yogurt I bought."

"Vanilla?" she asked, hopeful.

"Plain."

"You're killing me, Mayor." And with that com-

ment the tense mood and stilted conversation eased.
It hadn't taken much to get them there.

"I can't risk getting old and fat or having a heart
attack like Dad." His smile faded and so did hers.

"Your father had a heart attack?"

He confirmed with a nod. "Surgery, too. He's in
good health now, but it rattled me to see him in a hospital bed."

"Enough that you cut out three-cheese omelets."

"I indulge sometimes."

"I didn't accuse you of anything." She held her
hands up.

"No, but you're looking at me like I'm as bland as
the yogurt I mentioned."

A smile played at the corners of his mouth but there
was a dash of sadness ghosting his expression. Like
he cared what she thought of him.

Impossible. He was the most independent, self-
assured man she'd ever known.

"I have a surprise for you," he said, standing from
the couch.

"Oh? Did you lie about the Froot Loops?"

"Sorry. No." He bypassed the love seat where she
sat and opened a tall cabinet on the other side of the
room. On the shelves sat folded blankets, a few decorative pillows and board games. He closed the doors
and turned back to her, holding a familiar oblong box.

"Monopoly?" The box appeared brand-new, though
it wasn't wrapped in from-the-factory plastic.

"I was poking around while you were in the shower
and found this, Risk and Battleship." He set the game
on the coffee table and, after moving his wine to the
side, lifted the lid of the box. "I had no idea there were

games here. The house was stocked and decorated by a design team when I bought it. Wanna play?"

"Didn't you refer to that game as the 'ender of relationships'?"

"I did. But our relationship has already ended, so what's the harm?" His gaze warmed when he added, "Or maybe it'll have the opposite effect and we'll end up sharing a bed while you're here."

A startled laugh emerged from her throat. It was part *he's insane* and a sliver of *how fun does that sound?* The latter scared her more than a little.

"More wine before we start?" he asked as if he hadn't casually mentioned them sharing a bed.

"Water." No way was she drinking more alcohol tonight given the dangerous bend of her thoughts.

He returned from the kitchen with two bottles of water, sat down and raised his eyebrows. "What do you think?"

What did she think? All sorts of interesting, steamy, forbidden thoughts rolled around in her head. Chase. Hot, thirty-six-year-old Chase. With that smooth voice and slow hands—an attribute she recalled too clearly. He knew how to take his time. He'd been able to draw her to the brink of orgasm and let her linger there until she begged for release. Even at the tender age of twenty-three, she'd known that the sex was unparalleled. And when she'd ventured into dating a year later, she learned she was right. No one that she'd dated or slept with held a candle to the man sitting across from her bathed in firelight.

What tricks had he learned since then? A delicious shiver trickled down her spine.

"Scared?" he asked, mistaking her shudder of pleasure.

Terrified. Not of him but of her lack of willpower where he was concerned.

"Don't be," he continued. "I haven't played in years. You'll probably own my ass faster than I can say Marvin Gardens."

The game! Right. Not sex. She snapped the lid off her water and drank a few guzzles.

"If you're sure you can take me," she told him. "Bring it."

An hour and a half later, it was clear that she was going to lose.

Chase had monopolies with hotels on the scariest properties—not the blue ones. Park Place and Boardwalk were the obvious choices because of their price tags, but that wasn't how you won the game. No, the way to won was to buy up the yellow, orange and magenta properties so that in between the jail square and the go-to-jail square you would be fined into bankruptcy. Even owning all of the utilities and two railroads couldn't get her out of this mess.

"You're about to forfeit," he pointed out. "I can tell by the crease right there." He leaned forward and pressed the pad of his finger into the dent between her eyebrows. She slapped his hand away.

He was sitting on the couch at the long side of the coffee table and she'd sat opposite him on a big square cushion. Her dwindling pastel-colored dollars didn't inspire hope, but as far as forfeiting…

"Never." She narrowed her eyes and he grinned.

"Very well." He set the dice on the board without

rolling his turn and purchased several more houses. Then he rolled and landed on Boardwalk, a property he already owned.

Miriam was in "jail" and rolled for the third time, trying for doubles so she didn't have to pay the precious fifty-dollar fine to leave. She didn't *want* out. Not with all those plastic houses and hotels Chase had built that were waiting to empty her bank account. If she rolled two fives, she could not only get out of jail free, but rest on Free Parking for a breather. And win the money in the middle—only forty dollars, but every little bit helped.

But fate was not smiling on the less fortunate today. She landed on Tennessee Avenue, the property where Chase had just added another house.

"Game." He remained where he was, elbows on his knees and awaited her concession.

"Game," she said through her teeth.

He started filing away his money and she did the same, which took her a lot less time than it took him since she had so very little of it. By the time she was sweeping the houses off the board, she could feel the frown between her eyes deepen.

A low chuckle punctuated the air.

"What's so funny?"

"Nothing." He licked his lips as he helped organize the cards into stacks. "You're not a gracious loser, Mimi."

"No one likes to lose, *Chase*." Some of the fire went out of her voice, though. He looked genuinely relaxed and happy and it was hard not to replicate his mood. It was obvious from the faint lines between his dark eyebrows that he typically worried more than he relaxed.

Game boxed, he stood and put it away. When he paced back, he offered a hand to help her off the cushion on the floor. She accepted, his warm fingers curling around hers and making other parts of her warm, as well. Naughty, tingly parts. Oft-ignored parts.

She tugged her hand away and he tossed the square cushion she'd been sitting on onto the chair.

"Do you have everything you need for the evening?" he asked.

A jerky nod was all she could manage in response.

He lifted his hand to her cheek and brushed the back of his fingers from her jawline to her neck. His mouth pulled flat.

"I wish things wouldn't have ended so poorly between us, Mimi."

Her heart, her damned heart, dusty from being ignored for so long, thudded with regret.

"So do I," she admitted.

He gave her shoulder a gentle squeeze, his eyes on hers, his head tilted at the right angle for a kiss. Not that she should be kissing Chase Ferguson, but if he leaned in…*oh yes*, she'd kiss him. She'd kiss the life out of him if for no other reason than to learn if her lips still fit against his like they were made to.

They did. She knew it.

Instead of bending for a kiss, he returned both hands to his pockets. The heat in his eyes banked.

"There was nothing I could do at the time except wish you well."

The words stung like a rubber band snapped against her skin. They also snapped her back to reality. There was a warm fire and wine and casual, fun banter, but there was also ten years of loss and pain that separated them. A mountain that, while scalable, wasn't worth risking her heart to climb.

"Nothing you could do?" She threw his words back at him, mentally lacing up her hiking boots to climb anyway. "You put me on a plane the same day you brought me to Dallas. You didn't even offer me a place to sleep."

"Why would I have offered to take you home with me?" His expression was genuinely sincere.

"Because—" *I loved you* "—it was the decent thing to do!"

His face remained blank, his voice calm while she'd entered the lower range of yelling. "It would've been *decent* to break up with you and then invite you back to my bed? You were upset. You needed to go home where you belonged. Holding you while you cried wouldn't have eased the transition for either of us."

She wanted to scream or slap him. Or both. Instead, she welded her back teeth together and forced a breath through her nose. This was an old argument. One that couldn't be resolved then and sure as hell wouldn't be resolved if they talked about it now.

She hadn't seen Chase sending her away as *decent*. Especially after a flight where they'd made love in the private plane's cabin and he'd told her he was glad she'd come with him to Dallas. At the time she'd believed what they had was real and lasting, and she thought he'd believed that, as well.

Until dinner with his parents ended after Eleanor

had made her opinion abundantly clear. Chase had dumped Miriam right there in the driveway.

The memory stung like a cloud of angry wasps...

Nine

"*My mother's right,*" *Chase said from the driver's side of a sleek black Porsche. Miriam was still getting used to this much finery...and getting used to learning that his family owned an oil company. Like, one of the biggies.*

"*Right about what?*" *She stopped digging through her purse for her Chapstick and regarded him.*

"*Right about my career. I hadn't been thinking about it this summer.*" *He faced her, his expression tender, his voice low and filled with regret.*

She felt the hard kick of her heart against her ribs and forced a smile. Reaching for his hand, she said, "She's not right. She's wrong. You're going to be an incredible politician and no one, especially Mimi Andrix from Bigfork, Montana, is going to hold you back. The public will see us together and know what we have is real. How could anyone miss it?"

Squeezing his hand, she kept the smile on her mouth but he continued to look distraught.

"I wish that was true." He pulled his hand away and wrapped his fingers around the steering wheel. "Unfortunately, the position I'm in with my parents owning one of the biggest oil conglomerates in the state, I'm not at liberty to push back on any of this. My responsibilities to them, my interests in politics— having a say about how the people are treated in my city—matter."

She wanted to ask him if she also mattered, but was half afraid of the answer. It was like his mother had slapped a script in his hand. This wasn't Miriam's Chase. Her Chase had stripped her out of her dress and made love to her long and slow on a private jet hurtling them toward Texas. Her Chase had lain in that same bed and told her how beautiful her body was, before placing a kiss on each part he mentioned.

"You're scaring me," she confessed.

"We can't know so soon." His lowered eyebrows communicated regret at the words coming out of his mouth—words echoed from his mother, who'd said that exact phrase at dinner. "What happens from here on out, Mimi?"

She swallowed past the lump in her throat threatening to choke her. "What do you mean?"

"Do you move here from Montana? Leave your family? Marry me? What happens when I run for governor or mayor in the future? What happens when my opponent digs up proof you experimented with pot or a girlfriend in college? Or if we find out someone has

photos of the night we skinny-dipped in the lake? Or made love on the shore?" he added darkly.

"I don't care about any of that." Her voice took on a desperate quality, but she didn't care. In no way would she entertain this line of thought. What they'd shared in her hometown wasn't tawdry or dirty. It was beautiful—the start of their forever. *"I care about you."*

"You'll care when the press involves your parents. Your siblings. When a smear campaign starts and—"

"You're borrowing trouble, Chase. Right now, you're finishing law school. You could end up working for Ferguson Oil the rest of your life."

"And that would be okay with you?" He drilled her with a look that roiled her stomach. She'd never been a fan of the corrupt oil monopolies, but neither could she deny that she loved Chase too much to let his family ties keep her from him.

"I care about you, too," he said, and she heard the unspoken *"but"* that was about to follow. *"Too much to let you go down this road."* He captured her chin between his thumb and forefinger. Hot tears rolled from her eyes and scalded her cheeks. *"Let's slow down. Think things through."*

"There's nothing to think about!" Her shout was shrill in the closed interior of the car. It was September in Texas and plenty warm. The AC blew gently against her face, chilling the trails her tears left behind.

"We didn't think at all this summer," he said, gaze once again on the windshield. *"I didn't think."*

The argument had escalated from there, Chase closing off and her growing more emotional. Before she knew what was happening, he was on the phone with the pilot who'd flown them in earlier that day.

"Good night, Chase," she said now, her mind on that fated night, her voice rigid from spent grief and too many regrets to count.

There were so many things they should've said. So many things they *shouldn't* have said. Once, she'd considered him her everything, and now he felt as remote as a desert island.

But none of that mattered anymore. He'd made his decision to toss what they had aside, and she'd boarded the plane home willingly.

Memories weighing down her limbs, she trudged to her bedroom—toward the sweet relief of an empty mattress, and away from Chase's hurtful words—to be alone with her heart that still mourned the loss of what could've been.

Chase propped his hands on his hips and dropped his head back, studying the ceiling, or perhaps seeking advice from the Almighty.

"Got anything?" he asked the beamed ceilings.

No answer.

He hadn't meant to traipse down bramble-strewn memory lane. He'd meant to tell her that now that she was here, in his house, he wanted her in his bed again. He was going to follow that up with a promise that she'd never regret saying yes.

They should at least be kissing, if not half-naked, his lips wrapped around her nipple, his fingers in her underwear.

They should be exorcising the demon that had been unleashed, not arguing about why it existed at all.

Nostrils flared in frustration, he forced himself to stop thinking. He'd done too much thinking already. He followed the path Mimi had taken to her bedroom and stopped outside the door, fist raised to knock.

Before he could rap on the wooden panel, it opened. Mimi jolted in surprise. She wasn't expecting him. He lowered his hand, keeping it balled into a fist at his side.

"Hi," he said.

"Hi." She folded her arms over her small breasts. "I forgot to grab a bottle of water. I like to keep one on the nightstand." Her eyes flitted to the side, making him wonder if she was telling the truth.

"I didn't mean to hurt you back then."

He hadn't wanted to send her home. He'd selfishly wanted to take her home with him and soothe her. Stroke her hair and tell her everything would be okay. But there'd been no way to know if *anything* would be okay. There'd been no way to know she wouldn't wind up hating him for dragging her away from her life of pine trees and shorelines and into one teeming with politicians and oil tycoons. Keeping her at his side would have been about him, and he had forced himself to think of her—of who he'd have to ask her to become if she stayed.

She'd loved him then. He'd foolishly thought she'd continue loving him through her heartbreak. Long enough for them to see how his career would shake out. Long enough for her to decide for sure if she wanted to be a part of that life.

"I hate that I hurt you, but I had to—"

"Don't. Don't say that you had to focus on your career or your business or any other multitude of things that were more important than me at the time."

His scowl hardened and not in his own defense. He had done that. But he'd done it to protect her. *For her.* Evidently she wasn't ready to hear that.

"I can take care of myself, Chase. You don't need to worry about me now. I'm a big girl, and I'm not afraid of bad publicity."

"That's because you haven't been the target of it. You don't know what they'll say about you to get to me. I'd lose the election after the press learned I was beating the hell out of anyone who verbally attacked you."

He'd expected at least a half smile in response to that, but he didn't get one.

"I agreed to leave that day. It's not like you tied me up and dragged me into the plane."

"You only agreed to leave because I asked you to." Regret wasn't a familiar feeling, but it took residence in the center of his chest now. "I pushed you away."

Her dark eyes swept up to meet his. "It would be a hell of a lot easier to blame you for everything, but the truth is…" She licked her lips before she finished. "I was starting to wonder if I was right about us or if I'd been caught up in the fantasy. I didn't want to lose you, but I didn't want to leave Montana. In the car when you were shattering me—and make no mistake, Chase, you shattered me—"

He winced, hating hearing it but knowing it was true.

"—I was courting second thoughts." She laid her palm softly against his sweater and her warmth eased the sting of her words. "I can't let you shoulder all the blame. The lion's share maybe, but not all."

Instinctively, he cupped her hand with his own. The speed of his breaths increased, his heart rate ratcheting up along with them, a thumping they could both feel.

"This is so dumb," she said, her voice barely above a whisper.

He stepped closer, his other hand wrapping around one petite shoulder. He wasn't sure if she meant that talking about their past was dumb, or considering kissing him was dumb. Either way...

He ducked his head, pleased when she lifted hers to receive the kiss he was angling toward her plush mouth. In the split second before he closed his eyes, he watched her lids sink and felt the soft tickle of her breath against his mouth.

Their lips touched, his firm and solid against hers pliant and giving. He gentled her open and stroked the tip of her tongue with his. A sigh of longing mingled with loss coated his mouth when he moved to deepen the kiss, and that was the instant Mimi pulled away.

She lowered from her toes to her heels, eyes still closed, hand still on his sweater—now bunching the material.

"Dumb," she whispered again.

"Oh, I don't know. It wasn't so bad."

That earned him the hitch of her mouth: the smile he'd been gunning for. He swept her dark hair aside, the waves silky and oh-so-touchable.

"I've been thinking of kissing you since the day I saw you at the supermarket," he said.

Her eyebrows lifted like she was amused. "That would've been awkward."

"Timing is everything." He took a breath and spoke the words he'd wanted to say all night. "I swear, Mimi. If you come to my bed tonight, you will not regret it."

His voice was low and lethal, tight with the sexual tension that had strung his balls to his spine like a cable car.

Her expression shuttered. She yanked her hand away.

Too soon.

"Hang on. That's not—" He tried to backtrack but she cut him off.

"Let's pretend that last part didn't happen."

He braced his hands on the doorframe, effectively blocking her in as he leaned close to say, "Not what I was going to say."

She ducked under his arm and walked down the hallway toward the kitchen. He turned his head, resting his cheek on one outstretched arm to watch her go. Those round hips swishing away from him, her hair bouncing halfway down her back.

Damn.

Damn.

Ten

Outside Miriam's bedroom window, snow fell as hard and fast as ever. It was a beautiful inconvenience—a minor interruption in what was an already amazing life. She had much to be thankful for. Something she'd tried to remind herself last night while she lay awake feeling complete FOMO about missing out on Black Friday shopping with her sisters.

It wasn't the shopping itself she was mourning, but the time she'd miss spending *with them*. Dining out and then grabbing lattes for dessert. Juggling the to-go cup and a plethora of shiny shopping bags while one of them dug the keys from Wendy's purse so they could find the car.

She'd tried to reach either Kristine or Wendy on their cell phones. No luck. There were probably wrestling a discount television away from a grown man at a big box store, or maybe they'd opted for an early breakfast complete with mimosas.

After sending a group text—Buy me something of high value with a low price tag!—and tossing the phone on the bed, Miriam pulled on her jeans and layered a few long-sleeved shirts for warmth.

The house was cozy. The bed was a dream. She'd slept great once she'd finally fallen asleep.

When she'd returned to her room with the water bottle, Chase had no longer been looming at her doorway looking sexy and slightly rumpled and thoroughly kissed. He'd gone upstairs, she'd assumed. The house was large enough he could've been literally anywhere save the room she'd just come from. He hadn't said goodnight.

She'd lain in her bed and wondered if he was in his own bedroom reliving the smoldering lip-lock they'd shared in the doorway. If he still tasted her on his tongue the way she tasted him on hers. If he was considering coming back downstairs to sample her mouth again…

But he hadn't.

And now that she was awake and en route to the coffee maker, she tried to convince herself she was glad he hadn't come downstairs to finish what he'd started. Relaying those thoughts to her heart was easy. Getting them past her raging hormones and that irritating fluttering at the V of her thighs was another matter altogether.

It'd been a while since she'd had sex. It'd been even longer since she'd had really *good* sex. It made sense that the physical reactions in her body were shouting *Hell yes*! Her nipples had hardened and pressed against the T-shirt she slept in, begging for attention. She'd resisted the urge to relieve that pounding pulse between her legs herself, balling her fists in the blankets and squeezing her eyes shut. She thought about camp budgets and depleting rain forests and other unpleasant topics, but no matter how she'd tried to distract herself, memories of Chase—from last night and ten years ago—led the pack.

It was simply *him*. He had commanded her full attention since the first time she laid eyes on him. There was a pull surrounding him and whenever she was in his atmosphere she couldn't keep from being drawn in.

"As evidenced by my ending up snowed in here," she said to herself. What other than the idea of Chase Ferguson alone on Thanksgiving would have convinced her to come out in a snowstorm?

She paced to the kitchen, located the coffee and made herself a single-cup serving. After only three hours of sleep, she needed it. No sign of her housemate yet, but she could guess he hadn't slept well either.

She opted to give herself a tour of the house while sipping her coffee. She started with the main floor, most of which she'd familiarized herself with last night. The living room where they'd played Monopoly, the kitchen where Chase had heated his delivered dinner, and of course, her bedroom.

She'd had a peek at the other larger bedrooms dotting the halls when looking for her own, and took another gander now to be sure she was happy with her choice. She was. She'd chosen the smaller room because it was close to the kitchen and because it had a bathroom attached. Her idea had been to hide out until the storm blew over—the literal snowstorm and the one brewing between her and Chase. A cowardly plan. There was no escaping the blizzard just as there was no avoiding what had happened last night.

Upstairs she found a sitting area surrounded by bookshelves. A chessboard stood on a side table with two straight-backed chairs. She could imagine Chase hunched there, a wrinkle of consideration on his forehead, his fingers resting against his mouth while he thought of his next move. The room suited him, but the shelves on the walls—with a few generic leather-bound books and a random vase or decorative bowl taking up the empty space—appeared more what his decorator had deemed appropriate and less what Chase would've chosen for himself.

The library's window, pointed at the top to match the pitch of the roof and as wide as the room itself, looked over the deck at the back of the house and the snow-covered lake beyond. Natural light flooded in, but even the sun felt cold, too far away to melt the ice clouding the glass. In a pair of comfy sneakers, she stepped silently across the shining hardwood floors. A doorway beckoned her, the edge of Chase's bed in plain view, his own sneakers standing at the foot of that bed.

Light choked this space, streaming in from more floor-to-ceiling windows where the bed faced. His comforter had been thrown over the bed in a half-assed attempt at making it, two pillows stacked on one side. Jeans and a button-down shirt were draped over the bed like he'd been about to put them on but decided against it.

Where is he?

She stepped deeper into the room and ran her hand over the cream-and-dark-blue quilt, her fingers grazing the sleeve of his shirt. She could picture him here. Last night. Right now…

"Having regrets about what room you chose to sleep in last night?" a voice asked from behind her. She placed her hand over her heart in an attempt to slow its speeding rhythm.

"You startled me," she said breathlessly.

Facing him didn't help her catch her breath. He was shirtless, barefoot and water rolled in rivulets down his naked chest. He held a royal blue towel over his hips, grasped with one hand.

"You're wet," were the only words she could think to say. The only two words that eked from her suddenly parched throat. The only appropriate words she could've said out loud—and even those didn't sound appropriate. Her eyes feasted on the dark hair whirling on his chest, the trail of it leading down his flat belly and disappearing into the terry cloth around his hips.

Yeah, there were no words.

"I went for a swim. Finished it off with ten minutes in the hot tub." He stepped into the room with her and she felt the steam coming from his damp skin. "You should try it."

He ripped off the towel to expose he was wearing absolutely nothing at all. She jerked her eyes away and tried desperately not to replay the vision of the inviting appendage hanging temptingly between his legs.

Chase strolled toward his attached bathroom, not the least bit shy as he dried his arms and chest and his bare ass. She didn't mean to stare. It just…sort of happened on its own.

He had a round, firm butt leading to thick thighs that planed up to a defined, muscular back. His shoulders were strong, his traps defined...

He continued dressing, talking to her as if putting on clothes in front of an audience was a regular occurrence.

"I checked the weather this morning." He snapped the waistband of his boxer briefs and then tugged a T-shirt over his fabulous chest. "We're expecting another six to eight inches today." She didn't mean to look down when he said that, but she did and he noticed.

With a grin, he continued, "Another four to five inches tomorrow and possibly another two to three the day after that."

Covered in jeans and a T-shirt, he wasn't any less tempting than three seconds ago. He slipped his arms through a blue button-down a shade lighter than the towel he'd discarded on the floor. And now that her brain was working again...

"When do they expect to dig us out?" she was able to ask.

"There's no talk of digging anyone out, but there's an emergency service hotline if anyone is without heat or food. Both of which we have at the moment. The problem occurs when the snow becomes too heavy for the power lines."

"But you have a generator." She didn't bother putting a question mark on the end of that sentence—the alternative sounded too unpleasant.

"It's on the fritz." He finished buttoning his shirt. He left the top two buttons undone like she remembered. "We have fireplaces all over the house. We won't freeze."

"I can take a look at it."

His face flinched into an expression of disbelief. "I took a look at it yesterday. The gas tank's full, but it won't kick on."

"Yes, but I know how to repair a generator. Do you?" She propped one hand on her hip and sipped her coffee, letting that new detail sink in.

"Not particularly."

"I've repaired one before. And don't make a joke and ask if I brought my pink toolbox."

"Hopefully it won't come to that." He sat to pull on his socks and slipped his feet into shoes he didn't have to tie. "Again, I'm tempted to ask who the hell you've been dating. I'd never ask you if you have a pink toolbox. You hate pink."

He remembered, and that made her smile.

When he stood, he stepped closer to her, smelling woodsy and fresh rather than like chlorine. He looked as delicious wearing clothes as he did out of them. Unbelievable.

"May I?" He held out a hand for her coffee mug and she gave it to him. He took a sip, swallowed and closed his eyes to let out a soft "ahh" before handing her mug back. "I swam before I indulged. That tastes incredible."

She bet he did, too.

See? It was thoughts like that she needed to eradicate. Neither should she swoon because he'd remembered she hated pink.

"Um. Sorry to intrude," she said belatedly. "I wanted to check out the rest of the house."

"No intrusion." His voice slipped into a seductive husk that she'd started accepting was simply his normal speaking voice. "You're always welcome in my bedroom."

"Very funny, Mr. Mayor." She forced a droll tone.

"Can't blame me for trying." He smiled, his gaze fastened to hers and for a moment she wanted to say to hell with dancing around each other. She wanted to suggest they rid themselves of any restrictive, unnecessary clothing and make love on his massive bed while the snow fell and the wind howled. They could spend the rest of the day—*the week*—buried under thick quilts and silky sheets, leaving the room for food or drink. And only then to restore their spent energy so they could twist up the bedding again. Instead, she said nothing.

"The coffee is tempting. You're even more so." He drew her chin up with a knuckle and she got lost in the greys and greens of his irises. "But if I can't have one, I'll take the other."

Eleven

"Grilled cheese isn't the same without a ripe, red tomato." Chase turned with a plate of grilled cheese sandwiches—three of them. They were toasted to golden, gooey perfection, and Miriam's mouth watered. "Especially if it's from Texas."

"You brought tomatoes from Dallas?"

Red fruit in hand, he gestured to her with it. "I wasn't sure I could trust Bigfork's produce department." He set the tomato on a cutting board and cut it into thick slices. "Couldn't risk it."

"What happened to your accent?"

"Accent?"

"Yes," she said with a dose of sarcasm, "you know, the one you were taught in the great state of Texas."

"You prefer it?"

"No," she lied. "Just curious."

He flashed her a brief smile, one that made her wiggle in the seat she'd taken at the island.

"Well, darlin', if you want me to lay it on thick for you I can do that." He gave her a wink. "Real thick."

Rapt, Miriam twirled her hair around her finger, her other elbow resting on the island's countertop. The second she noticed she was doing it she folded her hands in front of her.

She shouldn't prefer his accent. It reminded her of being young and carefree and…stupid.

Stupid is the word you're looking for.

"Voice coaches," he said in an accent-free timbre. "Years of them. It creeps in every once in a while, when I let my guard down."

Something he rarely did, she imagined. Everything Chase did seemed intentional.

Coming here. His career. Dumping her.

"No tomato on my grilled cheese sandwich. I'm a purist. Just cheese."

He'd made the sandwiches with reckless abandon; three types of cheese oozed onto the plate from the center of the diagonally cut stacks.

"You don't like tomatoes?" He put a few thick slabs in between the bread of his own sandwich.

"I do—I just don't want them on my grilled cheese."

"Suit yourself."

"Do you have any pickles?"

"Sadly no. It's tomatoes or bust. I thought you were a purist."

She picked up a triangle. "There's nothing purer than a pickle on a grilled cheese sandwich."

If the crunch of the toasted bread wasn't enough

to send her into blissful abandon, the gooey, stringy cheese would've done it.

Chase lifted a half and took a bite. After he was done chewing he continued. "Damn. That is good. But no more moaning from you unless I elicit that response."

Her mouth was full so she had to finish chewing and sip her water before she responded.

"Okay. I feel like we have to talk about the kiss." She dusted her fingers onto a paper napkin.

"Okay." He continued eating, gesturing for her to go ahead.

"You can't kiss me and expect me to reciprocate."

"You *did* reciprocate."

"Going forward." She karate chopped the air in front of her. "You can't kiss me going forward."

"That's entirely up to you. But you can't stop me from trying to seduce you."

Shock unhinged her mouth. He was trying to seduce her?

"Are you trying to seduce me?"

"Do you think I trot out my famous grilled cheese for any woman? No, ma'am," he said, his accent creeping in. "Only one who is willing to tromp through Bigfork's worst snowstorm in a decade to bring me pie." He picked up the other half of his sandwich.

"I'm being serious."

"All right." In a blink, he'd dialed down the charm and upped the intensity. "Let's be serious."

He polished off that half in three big bites, took his time chewing and swiped his mouth with a napkin. Once he'd swallowed a generous amount of water, he flattened his hands on the island where he stood across from her and leveled her with a look.

Miriam was beginning to panic and had no idea where to settle her gaze. On him wasn't safe, but was by far the most appealing.

"You came here for a reason," he said. "What was it?"

"I told you. To set you straight. And, as you concluded, to make sure you ate a decent Thanksgiving dinner."

"What's under that, Mimi?" His tone was serious, his expression patient. "What is this?"

He gestured between the two of them and she could only assume that by *this* he meant the thrumming sexual attraction saturating the air. Since the kiss last night *that* had picked up where it'd left off years ago.

He offered her another half of a grilled cheese. She accepted, but didn't take a bite.

"Okay, fine," she admitted. "Yes, there's something here. But nothing we can act on."

"Why not?"

"Um, in case you don't recall, we failed miserably the first time."

"We won't make the same mistakes this time around. We're older and wiser. I have no accent now. Totally new experience."

Now, see? When he did that she wanted to argue that she wasn't interested in a second "time around" and assure him as much as herself that she didn't want to reexperience him...

But while her head was absolutely clear on that direction, her body was melting into a puddle. Chase was an experience—a fantastic one if memory served.

And *fantastic* hadn't been an adjective she'd used to describe anyone who had graced her bedsheets since the man standing across from her.

"Whatever you say, Mr. Mayor." She laced her words with sarcasm and offered a laugh.

Then she took another bite—a big one—so that she wouldn't have to give him an answer.

Mimi was putting up a good front, Chase would give her that.

Reading people was a talent he'd honed. It's what made him a great politician. And since he knew how to read people, he could tell that as much as Ms. Andrix was protesting this truckload of sexual attraction, she also wanted to test the boundaries between them.

Last night her body had responded to his when he'd kissed her. She'd held on to him like he was the only thing keeping her from floating off the ground. But he had to be careful in his approach. Schmoozing her wouldn't work, and neither would plying her with wine to lower her inhibitions. Inhibitions weren't her problem—she'd been plenty bold with him before.

She was nothing like the women who'd been in and out of his life over the past several years. Mimi had never been impressed with his money or his status. If anything, those were in his *con* column. No, when it came to her, his only choice for getting to the yes they both wanted was brash, flat-out honesty. That, he could do.

"The sex would be good," he told her. "Probably great but I couldn't commit to that adjective until after." He grabbed a bag of potato chips from the pantry, giving her a moment to absorb what he'd said. When he turned back, her eyes were wide with amusement.

"Is that so?" Done eating, she sagged on the barstool and folded her arms over her chest.

"I'm not playing with you, Mimi. It's not my style. I'm letting you know where I stand. If you change your mind about having sex with me, let me know. I'll have you out of those tight jeans and into my arms before your next breath. Either you'll give me the opportunity to show you how serious I am about making you feel incredible, or you'll refuse me until it stops snowing." He looked to the window where it appeared it would never stop snowing. "Those snowflakes are the sand in our hourglass. Eventually, they'll stop falling and then our time will be up."

"I'm aware of what our time being up feels like." Her expression was not one of hurt, but resolve. It was no surprise that she'd be cautious where he was concerned, a fact he'd overlooked until just this second.

"Guess when I implied you'd been dating some real winners, I didn't factor in myself, did I?"

Some of the fire swept out of her and her mouth lifted on one side. "That was a long time ago."

"You wear your heart on your sleeve. You always have. Meanwhile, I keep mine in a cage locked in a vault at the bottom of a dormant volcano."

That brought forth a closed-mouth smile but he felt pride knowing she was fighting a grin.

"I'm sorry."

Her smile swept away. "Don't…"

"I'm sorry I hurt you and put you on a plane to Montana ten years ago. It was all so…"

"Juvenile."

"No," he argued, meaning it. "Yes, we were young, but what we had wasn't meaningless. And it wasn't juvenile." He raised an eyebrow. "Pursuing you now isn't about my being an opportunist or checking off some bizarre sex bucket list. It's about you. And me. And what we could make of our time together."

"Scratch an itch?"

"Why not?"

"So, what is this conversation? A negotiation?" She smoothed her hands along the countertop in front of her. "Where's my contract?"

"It's an offer. Plain and simple." He lifted the plate where the last half of a sandwich sat. "More?"

"I couldn't. Thanks, though." A gap of silence followed. Chase lifted the sandwich half at the same time Mimi stood and backed away from the island.

"I'm going to turn in."

"At eight o'clock?"

"Yes." Her smile was tight. "Thanks for dinner."

"Sure."

She grabbed her water bottle and walked away, and every step had him growing more and more confused. Had he completely misjudged her interest? Had he said the wrong thing—the wrong *everything*? He'd gone into this day sure of his ability to convince her. Especially after she'd hungrily eaten him up with her eyes this morning.

His instincts pushed him to go after her, but he rooted his feet to the ground. Ten years ago, he'd worn her like a second skin day and night. She'd responded to his every touch and kiss by igniting in his arms. Pretending they could pick up where they left off wouldn't work.

He uncorked a fresh bottle of wine and poured himself a glass. He wasn't giving up, but it was time to change his strategy. She needed space, but he needed her.

They'd have to meet in the middle.

His eyes went to the snow—falling and filling in the gaps where he'd shoveled the deck this afternoon. He'd take as much time as Mother Nature would give him.

"Keep 'em comin'," he said to the wintry white sky.

Twelve

Miriam awoke to a scraping sound, which she'd grown accustomed to over the many winters she'd spent in living in Montana. It was the sound of a shovel sliding over concrete and sweeping the snow aside. She stretched her arms overhead and let out a shudder from the chill in the room. It was a touch colder in here than it'd been yesterday.

Last night she'd retreated to her room to think— or *not* to think, as it turned out. She'd pulled out her iPad and watched YouTube videos about yoga and how to truss a turkey. She'd watched makeup tutorials and learned how to build a "capsule wardrobe." She'd checked her social media and used her meditation app and played a colorful puzzle game on her iPhone. None of those distractions took her mind off Chase.

Or how she'd walked away last night when what

she'd wanted to do was say not just yes, but *hell yes* to his offer. He'd told her the truth about what he wanted, and she hadn't been brave enough to do the same for him.

"When did you become such a coward?" It wasn't like she could hide from him the entire time she was here.

She peeked through the curtains and saw that Chase did indeed own boots. He was wearing a pair, and hunks of snow covered his knit hat and black coat. He hefted another heavy shovel load and stopped to take a breather. How long had he been out there?

He looked cold, his face red from windburn, and the snow wasn't slowing. The area he'd cleared was already filling in with fresh flakes.

Well. She wasn't going to stay ensconced in her bedroom like a princess in a castle. She wasn't afraid of hard work. She layered a pair of yoga pants under her jeans and slipped her feet into two pairs of socks before pulling on her boots. By the time she buttoned her coat and stepped into the garage—after first *finding* the door to the garage in the massive house—she blinked in surprise at what she saw.

Not at Chase's new SUV, which he'd purchased after landing in Bigfork, but by what sat next to it. Her truck. He'd found her keys and then shoveled her out before parking her truck in a spot next to his. She skirted a puddle of melted snow, in search of a shovel to help him in his endeavors, kicking a gas can on the way. She nudged it with her boot. Empty.

He'd filled her tank.

She shut the cabinet and punched the button for the garage door, watching as it rolled up and revealed first a pair of tied boots, then snow-covered jeans and then his long wool coat. When the door sat at the top of its hinges, the rest of Chase was revealed—his breath visible from parted lips, a knit hat pulled snugly over his ears, snowflakes nestled in his thick lashes... Just the sexiest man alive.

"What are you doing?" she asked. "Shouldn't you be packing all that snow against the door to keep me here?"

He grinned, a puff of steam escaping his mouth. She joined him outside, the air blasting her face shockingly cold compared to the much warmer garage. The air iced her lungs, but she couldn't help admiring the view. She walked across the mostly cleared driveway, stopping short of the three feet of snow lining the edge to look out beyond the lake. Sturdy green pines were coated in snow, their limbs drooping from the weight. The lake was frozen—at least on the surface, and a gust of wind swirled the snow over it.

"Beautiful," she sighed.

"Gorgeous." Chase agreed, but when she looked back at him, his hand was resting on the shovel's handle, his eyes were unmistakably on her.

He broke the tender moment with, "I forgot how cold it is up here. Remind me to visit in the summer next time."

"You filled up my truck. You're clearing the driveway. Trying to get rid of me?"

"You know that's not true."

"I came out to help."

"I'm almost done."

"You should go in. The cold has a way of creeping up on you out here. You're not used to it." She slipped one glove off and touched his face. It was like the chilly air was embedded in his cheek. "You're freezing, Chase. Come inside and warm up."

Sensuality crept into her voice without her permission. She let the offer dangle while he watched her carefully.

"Will you build a fire for me?" she asked.

"Am I to believe that you, the wilderness woman, can't build a fire for yourself?"

"I can build a fire better than you can," she said, pulling her glove back on. "But I want you to do it for me. It'll help you warm up."

Without waiting for his answer, she turned and strolled through the garage, around their cars and back inside. To her everlasting satisfaction, he didn't stay outside to prove he could shovel the driveway. He followed her in.

Well, this is new.

Much as he hated to leave a task incomplete, he couldn't resist following Mimi inside for a couple of reasons. First off, she was right, he needed to warm up. He'd been out there so long his fingers were stiff and his legs felt like popsicles.

She hung her coat and tugged off her gloves. "I suggest you slip into something warmer before making that fire."

Like you? He kept that question to himself. What do you know? He was getting wiser.

"I'm going to change." She started down the hallway before pausing to ask, "How did you find my truck keys?"

"They were in your coat pocket." He gestured to the living room. "Now they're on the coffee table."

She uttered a noncommittal "Hmm" and then disappeared to "change" even though he thought she looked fine.

Ten minutes later, he was downstairs wearing a sweatshirt and running pants, his legs still so cold that the newfound warmth was almost painful.

"Coffee or tea?" Mimi called from the kitchen.

"Both. Either. Add some antifreeze." He knelt in front of the hearth, looking over his shoulder to catch her laugh, but she was facing away from him. A pair of tight skin-hugging pants rounded her bottom. He promptly forgot about building a fire. No need now that there was one flaming to life in his pants. Damn, she looked good. Those subtle curves more pronounced thanks to the stretchy material. He watched her backside while she reached for mugs and bent for spoons.

When she hid that fine ass behind the kitchen island, he went back to his work. Which was…what again? Oh, right. Making a fire.

"Coffee," she said when he'd bent to light the twisted newspaper. He accepted the mug and watched as flames licked along the bottom of the wood.

"Not bad." She reached in and adjusted a log. He snatched her hand away.

"Don't put your hand in there. It's on fire."

"It's not going to catch unless you allow some air between those logs. Fire needs air. Your stack resembles a log cabin. It'd be lucky to see a faint draft."

"Very funny." He handed her the wrought iron fire

poker. "Use this. I happen to like your fingers attached to your body."

She slid him a foxy little glare and he got out of her way. Her butt shook as she poked and prodded his handiwork. That sexy wiggle made him want to beg for mercy—or relief that could only come from her naked and lying against him.

"There you go." The fire was high and bright when she turned to face him. "I'll make a mountain man out of you yet."

"Sorry, honey. I'm a Texan first and foremost. But good luck with that." She moved to stand and he stayed her with one palm. "Stay put."

He pulled a folded blanket from the cabinet and tossed it to her. She spread it out on the rug in front of the fireplace and arranged a few pillows from the neighboring love seat on the floor.

He sat next to her and handed her a coffee mug, keeping his own in hand.

"Thawing out yet?" she asked, lifting her steaming mug to her lips.

"Finally." His eyes slid down her long legs, folded to one side. "I like those pants."

Her eyes widened, her lashes fluttering a few times.

"A lot." He punctuated that comment with a nod.

She threw her head back and laughed for a solid three seconds before sobering on a hum and sipping her coffee.

"Only you, Chase Ferguson."

"Only me what?"

"The consensus by most men is that a rail-thin brunette with dark eyes, sticks for legs and a practically nonexistent chest does *not* a pin-up girl make. Yet you look at me like…" She shook her head, seemingly at a loss for words.

"Like what?"

Her cheeks went rosy and her throat worked when she swallowed. "Like you used to."

She ducked her head, but no way in hell was he letting her ignore what was roaring between them. Not again. Not after she'd come outside to pull him in from of the cold.

"Like I know your calves lead from delicate ankles to the crooks of the sexiest knees I've ever laid my lips on?"

She remained silent, but her top teeth scraped her bottom lip. For a change, she didn't have a salty quip or sharp-tongued argument.

"Like I know your hair feels like silk, and every time you pull your fingers through the strands I remember what it felt like brushing against my thighs?"

Her fingers tightened around her mug and those big brown eyes kept on staring.

"Like I know flecks of green hide in your dark irises like bursts of light?" He set his mug on the coffee table and took hers from her now trembling hands. "I know that because I remember exactly what it was like to be nose to nose with you, Mimi. I remember what it felt like with your breath coasting over my lips, your eyes open and drilling into mine while I sank deep inside you."

He scooted closer, hearing her hectic intake of breath and practically feeling the pulse jumping at the side of her neck.

"Don't get me started on your mouth." His voice was a lust-soaked rasp. "Your lips were made for kissing."

Before he could say more, those kissable lips crashed into his.

He caught the back of her head with one hand, bracing himself with the other to keep them from toppling over. An instinct. If he'd had one millisecond to reason, he'd have laid on his back and pulled her on top of him.

Her lips slid over his, the tentative push of her tongue testing his willingness to open his mouth to hers.

Willing and able, sweetheart.

Thirteen

No memories came crashing back to her. There was only the present, only the way Chase's fingers felt cradling the back of her head. Only the way his rough jaw scraped her sensitive skin as he angled his mouth and kissed her deeply.

His tongue tasted of coffee and something else—something basal and carnal and undefinable. It was *him*. And every womanly part of her reacted without her brain's permission.

His fingers left her head and rested on her nape, his thumb stroking her jawline as his tongue plundered her mouth. High, desperate sounds of longing infiltrated the space between them and at first she didn't recognize her own voice.

It'd been a while since someone had kissed her with such…ownership. No, not ownership. *Familiarity*.

He knew her body. He wasn't lying about that. She'd thought ten years had dampened memories of what it was like to be held by him, but now that she was in his arms it was like no time had passed.

He moved his wide palms until they wrapped around her ribs. Heating the material of her shirt and then burning right through it.

"Chase."

He didn't respond, kissing her as he slid his hands south, fumbling with the edge of her sweatshirt and the T-shirt under it.

"Chase."

"Hush," he said at the same time he found her bare skin. She caught his face between her hands and met his eyes. Smoky green eyes filled to the brim with heat. Lust for her. This gorgeous man wanted her. She was insane for pretending she didn't want him right back.

"Do you—"

"Don't talk. No talking." He didn't give her a chance to, either. He lifted her sweatshirt and stripped it over her head, mildly perplexed to find another shirt in its place. When he reached for her T-shirt, she grabbed the edge and held it down.

"I don't remember you hurrying before."

"There are too many things I want to do to you and not enough snow falling to guarantee you will stay long enough for me to do them." He canted one eyebrow and regarded her with seriousness.

She decided to shut up and kiss him instead of having this conversation. It was best they didn't think too much about what they were doing. It'd been a long time since she'd been caught up in the rush of physical attraction. It was futile to resist him. She'd sought him out this morning and it had little to do with helping him shovel snow. She didn't like him being far away—she liked him close. Really close.

Skin to skin.

He molded his hands around her breasts, still encased in her bra and let out a low growl of approval. "Missed these."

It wasn't a *missed you* but close enough. She reached behind her back to unhook her bra strap. When the cups sagged, his eyes grew dark and hungry. She was in awe now like she'd been the first time she'd been naked in front of him. Amazed that this stunning specimen was so eager to make her his.

"Take it off."

She obeyed his command, letting the straps fall and reveal her breasts. He wasted no time leaning forward to capture one nipple on his tongue, his thumb sweeping over the other as he pressed his weight against her. Sensitive nerve endings shot pleasure down her arms and southerly. She fell back onto the blanket, his lips and tongue working their magic.

"You planned this," she panted, her hands raking into his hair. "That's why you gave me the blanket."

"Couches are for making out," he let her nipple go to say. "You and I have more room down here and we're doing more than making out."

She clucked her tongue at his assumption, but then he lowered his head again and she forgot about taking him to task. Her hands buried in his thick, dark hair, she savored the tug of his lips as sparks danced between her legs.

He swept his mouth to the other breast at the same

time his hands fisted the waistband of her yoga pants and tugged.

"Chase." Her moan was a frail breath, mingling with the sound of the crackling fire and her lost intentions.

He wrestled the stretchy material from her legs, socks with them, and then he began to strip himself.

Shoes went first, then his shirt. Then he shucked his pants and tore off his socks. She sat up on her elbows to watch the show. His quick, efficient movements revealing every inch of the man she was literally aching to look at.

He'd been leaner back then. He was still lean, but the muscles cording his arms and neck were heavier than she remembered. His chest was rounded—and her mouth went dry as she studied the hair swirling over his skin and marching a path down, down...

He climbed to his knees and her eyes went straight for the promise of what was to come. His cock hung heavy, erect, and she swallowed. That hadn't changed a bit—that part of him had always been impressive. Able to render her a boneless mass in record time while she called his name on a loud, sated shout.

"You remember," he growled, on his hands and knees over her. "I can see it." His lips brushed against hers. "You want me. Admit it."

It took her a moment to detach her very dry tongue from the roof of her mouth, but when she did she managed, "Egomaniac."

A deep, rough chuckle resonated against her chest. He pressed his lips to her shoulder for a kiss that was a promise of sinful things to come.

Her if she was lucky.

And with Chase, she'd always gotten lucky.

"Lie back," he said. "I have to taste that honey."

Her knees locked together, thighs squirming at his brazen offer. When she didn't obey right away, he turned his head gave her a serious side-eye, letting her know that complying was the only option.

She obeyed and he was over her instantly, lifting her head and sweeping aside her hair to place a pillow under her head.

"Keep in mind—" he paused to kiss her "—with your thighs locked around my head, I won't be able to hear as well." He kissed her again. "So, speak up. I don't want to miss a thing."

He took his time descending, kissing her collarbone, tonguing her nipples, flattening his palm on her belly. When he slipped his fingers along her damp folds, she nearly shot off the floor.

"Sensitive. I like that," he praised.

He lifted her right leg and she looked down at him hovering there, his lips pressing her inner thigh. He looked good there. Like he *belonged* there. He'd always fit her in every way—heart and soul, body and mind.

Was it any wonder she'd followed him to Dallas? She'd have followed him to the ends of the earth if he'd asked.

Those thoughts were zapped from her head the moment his mouth hit her sweet spot. She arched, heat blooming in her stomach and stretching out to numb her every limb. Chase was bathed in firelight, the orange glow hugging the contours of his perfect body.

He went down on her, moving like a feral animal and devouring her like a second Thanksgiving feast.

It was at once erotic and beautiful. Her nipples peaked and she reached for them, tenderly squeezing the buds and writhing in innate pleasure.

When Chase drew a cry of satisfaction from her lungs she didn't want him to ever stop. Her greedy body ached for another powerful release, but he didn't give her one, instead rising from the cradle of her thighs.

"So good," she said on a weak breath.

"I agree." He climbed her body, pressing his erection into the crook of her thigh. He nipped her earlobe. "You're delicious."

He nudged her again.

"Please," she begged, wrapping her ankles around him and pulling forward with all the strength she could muster. She was shameless. Absolutely shameless. Before she could get lost in the fullness of having him seated deep, her dormant brain kicked into gear. "Oh, God, Chase."

"I know, honey."

She almost laughed at the desperation in his voice. She grasped his face and forced his gaze to meet hers. "Tell me you have condoms."

The heat in his eyes banked as reality took a hard hold. Then his eyes sank closed and he muttered a devastating, "Shit."

"No." It was a weak plea to the otherwise cruel universe. How dare fate bring him to her and strand her in his house only to leave them moments shy of intense sexual satisfaction?

"Wait." His eyes flew open. "I had this house stocked before I came here. *Fully* stocked."

"Yes. I saw a bottle of Windex in the garage,"

she said, clinging to any scrap of hope that whoever thought to buy a bottle of Windex had also tucked a box of condoms into one of the medicine cabinets. It was a thin argument, but she'd take it. "Tell me they thought of everything."

He said nothing. She lost the warmth of his body a fraction of a second later when he stood.

"I'll help you look." She sat up.

"Don't move. I mean it." The shake in his arm when he pointed was almost comical. Almost. She wasn't laughing. She was too worried about there not being condoms in the house.

Please, God. Do me this one favor.

Before she could rationalize for or against praying for condoms, Chase stuffed his legs into his jeans and set off on a search of the house.

Fourteen

"Eureka." Chase had checked three of the four bathrooms before hitting pay dirt in the one near the downstairs bar. Good thing, too. He was freezing, which wasn't helping the situation due south.

Foil wrapper in hand, he started up the stairs before he thought better of it, turned back and grabbed the entire box. He'd need to keep these close for what he planned to do with Mimi tonight.

His feet like ice, he jogged upstairs and prayed she hadn't changed her mind. If she had, he wasn't above begging. He arrived in the living room and found her resting on her side, hand propping up her head, blanket covering her lower half. She'd waited like he told her. Triumph swelled in his chest.

Her dark hair flowed in waves over her back, a back he had full view of since she wasn't facing him.

His eyes traced her smooth skin, all of him vibrating to life in an instant. He wasn't cold any longer.

"Found 'em." He tossed the box of condoms onto the coffee table, keeping one within reach. She peeked over her shoulder and smiled, a drop-dead gorgeous still-frame he wouldn't soon forget.

He hastily undid his jeans and pushed them halfway down his legs. She rolled to her back, letting the blanket fall to the side, and revealed her small, perfect breasts. They'd tasted as good as she looked and he hadn't yet had his fill of those rosebuds.

"I was afraid you'd lose interest," she teased, a sparkle in her eye.

"That's my line," he teased back.

"I'll do the honors, Mr. Mayor." She swiped the condom packet from the table and tore it open with her teeth. His erection gave a happy bob. "But first..." She sat up on her knees, eye-to-eye with his...

Sweet mercy.

She took him in her mouth, softening her lips and opening wide to accommodate his girth. His hips tilted and thrust and she encouraged each pump by holding on to his thighs as she dove in again and again. One hand resting on the back of her head, he let out a harsh gust of air. His mind melted into a glob of indistinct thoughts for...he didn't know how long. When she finally robbed him of her mouth, he was hard as granite, his fingers tightly wound in her hair.

"God Almighty," he murmured—comically breathless.

Her eyes turned up to him, she licked her lips and took her time rolling the condom down his length.

"Where do you want me?" she purred.

He didn't hesitate. "Stand up."

She stood, her long, slim figure and subtle curves gliding along a narrow frame. He grasped her biceps and gave her a light squeeze.

"You've been working out."

"If you call working outdoors working out." She lifted her hands to his bare biceps. "Let me guess. From a gym?"

"And a personal trainer."

"Worth it. You're sexier than you used to be." She let out a soft laugh. He intended to show her exactly how much sexier he'd become by breaking her down, orgasm by orgasm, in a feat of animal, carnal lovemaking.

He cupped her nape and tilted her face, bending to kiss her lips. The kiss started tentatively but finished deep—their tongues tangling. Panted breaths burst from her lips as she rubbed her lithe, naked body against his.

His hips surged forward, his brains scrambling.

This woman.

No one unraveled him like she did.

He bent and lifted her until her legs wrapped around his hips, and then pressed her back to the nearest wall. She shrieked on contact.

"Cold!" Her nipples pebbled as goose bumps sprang to the surface of her skin. He bent and took a breast to task at the same time he positioned himself at her entrance and drove deep.

Her shriek of annoyance from the cold wall faded into a long moan of pleasure. One that he rode into the next thrust and the one after that.

Arms around his neck, she clawed at his shoulders,

bucked in response to his driving need. He buried himself not only in her body but in her scent, the soft strands of her hair sticking to his five o'clock shadow. Her blunt nails leaving marks on his skin.

"Come for me, honey," he said between labored breaths.

"Chase."

"I have you. I won't let you go." By that he meant he was supporting her and wouldn't let her fall, but the second it was out of his mouth it was obvious that where they were concerned, it had another meaning.

He'd said something similar to her ten years ago before he brought her home to Dallas.

I won't let you go.

He had, though. And now he'd been given a second chance, but he wouldn't make that promise again—he couldn't afford to break it again.

He tilted her hips and plunged into her again. She dropped her head back, her hair a messy tornado spread over the wall, her shoulders pressed flat, perky breasts begging for attention.

Attention he gave them.

It wasn't an easy move, but he managed thanks to his height. And it was that very move that sent her over, tumbling her into orgasm as she screamed his name with wild abandon.

Over and over she called, "Chase. Chase. Chase!" until his name faded into a contented sigh. Once she spent herself riding him, he allowed himself to let go of his own release, spilling inside her as his mind went blissfully blank.

Nothing mattered—not the past or the future— apart from the woman in his arms.

* * *

Miriam's limbs tingled like she'd been plugged into an outlet. Chase had her pinned to the wall, his forehead resting on her shoulder as his powerful back expanded with each ragged breath he took.

She was still impaled on him, loving the feel of him inside of her, his woodsy scent surrounding her. Loving his reaction when she'd taken him into her mouth before they'd started. His legs had shaken under her hands. The way she'd shaken when he took her against the wall.

I have you. I won't let you go.

She squeezed her eyelids closed to shut out his words. What they had was only physical—only an itch they'd chosen to scratch. Mimi and Chase were not "Mimi and Chase" of ten years ago, but adults who had agreed to sex and nothing more.

But the former her—the her who had loved him with everything in her twenty-three-year-old being—*wanted* to hold on to those words. To tuck them away because they made her feel warm and wanted.

She unhooked her legs from his waist and he pulled out, setting her feet on the ground. She sagged against the wall, her knees wobbly.

"Thanks, Mr. Mayor." She kept her tone cheeky and was pleased when her comment drew a dazzling, if tired, smile out of him.

"Does this tick a sexual fantasy box for you, Mimi?"

"Several." She counted them off on her fingers. "Wall sex. Mayor sex. Mansion sex."

His smile didn't budge.

He stole a quick kiss and he took a moment to visit

the half bath. She watched his firm butt flex as he walked, reminding herself to send a note of thanks to his personal trainer. He reemerged as she was settling in front of the fire, pulling the blanket around her body.

"I failed at warming you up," he said.

"You *ignited* me. It wore off." She held out her palms, soaking in what little heat was coming from the embers.

He tossed another log onto the fire and stoked the flames before sitting with her. "Do you approve?"

"I would think that was obvious."

"I was talking about the fire, but I'll take that compliment." He opened his arms and she nestled into him, his hands warming her through the blanket and making her toastier than the fire.

"How are you this hot?"

"So many ways to answer that question." He ducked his head to kiss her, a long, heady slide of his lips along hers. "Next time, we won't rush."

Next time.

Those two words swirled around her mind for a second. He thumbed her lip and pulled it out from under her top teeth.

"There *will* be a next time. I didn't mean for it to be over so soon, but it's been a while."

"A while?" She regarded him with raised brows.

He let her go, lying back on the floor with his hands behind his head. She admired the strong line of his body, the muscles along his torso and abdomen, the way his cock, even at half-mast, hadn't lost any of its appeal.

"Define a while."

"Longer than a jiffy." He winked.

"Har har."

His eyes closed and she watched the firelight play on his long dark lashes. Was it true? Was this powerful, gorgeous man single? Was he lonely? She sure as hell had been. Even when she'd dated, she'd suffered from bouts of deep, unmoored loneliness. The senselessness of her being lonely here and Chase being lonely there resonated in her chest. What could've been…

Is better off left unexamined.

"I'm starving. Coffee didn't cut it this morning." She'd said it partially to keep from asking him if he'd been lonely, and mostly to keep from talking about "next time." Ideas of "next time" made her hungry in an entirely different part of her anatomy.

"I like that smile." He tapped the edge of her lips. "I must've done well."

Was it her or had his Texas drawl taken hold again?

"Shameless begging for compliments will not get you any. But I will make you breakfast." She moved to stand, but he caught her arm with one hand and gently pulled her down.

"Brunch. It's almost eleven."

"We don't have brunch in Bigfork. It's *breakfast* and sometimes we eat breakfast for dinner."

"I remember."

Those two words settled in the air, simple but heavy. Proof that he knew her. Proof that he hadn't been a mirage. And what they'd just done together was proof that she hadn't imagined how good the sex used to be—dare she say it'd been better?

"You made pancakes one night." His smile was

reminiscent, his gaze soft. "Slathered them in peanut butter and called it dinner."

She smiled at the memory. "You thought I was crazy."

"No." He looked at her, his smile fading some. "I was crazy about you. You could have fed me anything on those pancakes and I'd have eaten them."

"We were crazy." She shook her head. The days they hadn't spent in the lake or on the beach or outside soaking in the summer sun, he'd been in her apartment—both of them wedged onto her twin bed against one wall of her bedroom. "My roommate complained so much about the noise we made, she was relieved when I followed you back to Texas."

"I remember that, too." His smirk was one of pride. He'd always loved being complimented on his prowess.

"Well. I promise no peanut butter pancakes. And eggs are out since you don't have them." She wrinkled her nose. "How can you not like a cheesy omelet?"

His mouth turned down. "Yuck."

"You sounded like my five-year-old niece just then."

"I have one, too. My niece is—" Pride pulled his lips into a smile. "She's amazing. So small and beautiful and…just amazing."

"How old is she?"

"Eleven months and change. Her birthday's on Christmas Day. We were in the middle of a family Christmas, complete with ugly sweaters when Zach's wife, Penelope, went into labor. I'll never forget Olivia's wide eyes and tiny fingers. Worth waiting for hours in the hospital for her to arrive."

"Pretty name." Miriam returned his smile. "My sister-in-law endured seventeen hours of hard labor and I spent most of it camped out in the cafeteria or the waiting room absolutely dying to know if she'd had a boy or a girl."

"She kept it from you."

"From all of us. It was brutal. But then I held Raven for the first time and felt this overwhelming...joy."

"I bet you're a great aunt." He pushed a lock of hair from her face.

She'd bet he was a great uncle. Pride mingled with protectiveness in his eyes.

Proving further that he took his job as uncle seriously, he said, "I told everyone that Olivia's gifts had to be wrapped in birthday-themed paper and not holiday wrapping paper. It's a big deal to have a birthday on Christmas. I mean, she shares it with Jesus. It should stand out."

An effervescent giggle shook her shoulders. This was what she'd fallen for when she'd first met Chase. His reasoning. His involvement. Just...*him*.

"My sister's girlfriend's birthday is on Christmas and Wendy reminds us every year that there's absolutely no cheating on the wrapping paper."

"I've decided if it's pink and makes noise, I'm buying it for Olivia. Serves Zach right for being a pain-in-the-ass little brother for most of my life."

She could imagine Chase hauling in loads of bubble-gum-colored glitter wrapping paper and stacking it around his tiny niece.

"Raven is a terror but I love her. And now I won't see her again *until* Christmas." A dart of pain pinched her chest. "They live in Virginia."

More snow fell outside, reminding her that she wasn't going anywhere soon.

"I'm sorry."

"Don't be." She'd called last night to check in on everyone. Her mother said they had "a dusting" of snow, but nothing that would trap them indoors. Miriam then spoke with Ross's wife, Cecilia, and Raven, and finally, Kris.

Kris had whispered *hold on* and Miriam had listened to light footfalls as she ran up the stairs. A few seconds later, after she'd escaped the family, Kris let Miriam have it.

What happened! Did you sleep with him yet? Are you in love with him again?

Miriam had answered a stern *no* followed by a sterner *seriously*? She'd also asked her sister if she'd recently taken up day drinking. Before they hung up, Kristine issued one last warning.

Don't let yourself get towed in by a sexy guy in a suit, Meems...but if you do, and who could blame you, make sure you enjoy yourself. No guilt allowed.

No guilt allowed.

In this moment, in front of a cozy fire with a naked, sinfully sexy man sprawled on the floor next to her... Snowed inside a luxurious mansion with anything and everything she could want... Yeah, it was safe to say her reigning emotion wasn't guilt. She had no problem taking what she wanted—what she'd needed.

Chase was stroking her arm, silent and thinking his own thoughts—whatever those were. She had a pretty good idea what they *weren't*. He wasn't thinking of the past or the future. His concern probably didn't extend beyond him enjoying himself and making sure she enjoyed herself in the scant amount of time they had left.

"You know, I have frozen waffles," he said, taking her hand and weaving their fingers together. "And maple syrup and bacon."

"And peanut butter?" She grinned.

"I'm a bachelor. *Of course*, I have peanut butter." He stood and pulled his jeans on and Miriam watched the way he moved, thinking he might be the devil in the flesh for all the temptation he offered.

"Can I help?"

"No. I need you to stay naked and save your strength. I can think of another use for the peanut butter besides slathering it onto waffles." He snagged his shirt off the floor.

She rolled her eyes but couldn't deny that she could think of another use for it, too.

Fifteen

"How come you're not married with a few of your own kids running around?" Chase asked.

"Excuse me? Did you just make a barefoot-and-pregnant reference about me?" Her eyebrows rose in offense.

"No." The word was outlined with patience. "I asked a question. We already covered the easy stuff. Time to answer a few hardballs."

She'd stayed naked like he'd requested while they ate waffles, but they'd since slipped back into their clothes, lounging on the couch after he threw another log on the fire. They'd chatted about college and the jobs they'd held after graduation. They talked about their siblings and their parents—he and Mimi were both close to their families. He hurt for her when she mentioned missing her late father. Chase knew too well how it felt to watch a parent have a close brush with the Other Side. He wished he could make a deal with the universe to keep Rider and Eleanor Ferguson immortal. His siblings, too. Hell, *everyone*.

The worry over his father's heart attack had eaten Chase alive, and if his dad had met his maker that day rather than coming out of surgery like the trooper he was, Chase didn't know what he'd have done. He'd steered them from that topic back to work. Mimi had spoken about the community as it applied to her working for Montana Conservation Society and he had discussed what it was like being mayor of a huge city. Like he said, easy stuff. Now the gloves were off.

"Tell me about the guy you last dated." He was sitting next to her on the couch and moved to stretch out. "And come here."

She made a frustrated sound in the back of her throat but came as asked.

"Guess I don't need that blanket," she said as she settled in next to him. "You're hot enough for both of us. And *yes*, I know how that sounds."

He smiled at her petulant tone. She wedged herself between the couch and him, and he wrapped his arm around her. Her palm resting over his heart, her cheek on her hand, she pulled in a contented breath. Contented, despite her trying her damnedest to resist him—or at the very least to keep him at arm's length.

He liked her here in his arms, her breasts pressing his chest, her breath tickling the hand that stroked her arm. He was aware that the trade-off for her being here was that she wasn't with her family. He didn't care. That might make him a selfish bastard, but in his defense, he hadn't seen or talked to Mimi in years and they'd seen her mere days ago.

"Who was he?" he repeated, curious to hear about the imaginary guy he'd concocted. In his mind Mimi's most recent ex had a protruding gut and did nothing but drool in front of his PlayStation while drinking cheap beer.

"Why do you want to know so badly?"

Because he wanted to know who he was up against, but he wasn't admitting as much. So instead he said, "Humor me."

"Gerard Randall. He's an environmental specialist for Yore Corp, a corn-processing plant south of Bigfork. I met him at a conference. We dated for eight months before we both admitted it wasn't working. We cut our losses and moved on." One of her slight shoulders lifted in a shrug.

Chase felt his mouth turn down. He liked his own story better. This Gerard Randall guy sounded moderately successful—not that Mimi would ever stoop to date the guy in Chase's imagination—and their split sounded amicable. Though that news was good. He didn't want her brokenhearted, tossed aside.

Like you tossed her aside.

"What about you? How come you don't have a wife and children?"

"My career keeps me busy," he answered automatically. It was the truth, but an exaggerated one. He wasn't too busy for a relationship. He hadn't found anyone he wanted to pursue.

"That answer was canned." She lifted her face to look at him and for a moment his breath snagged in his lungs. Not at her astute observation, but at her sheer beauty.

"You're so beautiful." He stroked her cheek with the pads of his fingertips. "I always thought so, but you've become more beautiful."

"Nice try. Who was she?"

"Who?" His brow crinkled.

"I told you who I last dated. It's your turn!" She poked him in the stomach.

"The *beautiful* comment won't save me that fate?"

"Nope." She overenunciated and popped the *p*.

"Darla McMantis."

Mimi squinted one eye. "Did you make that up? That sounds made-up."

"We were working on a don't-text-and-drive initiative for high schoolers at the beginning of this year. She's on the school board and wanted a face for the campaign. Mine."

"I'll bet," Mimi interjected, sounding jealous enough to make him smile.

"After we completed the plans, she asked me out for a drink. That drink was followed by a few dinners and two professional functions where she stood in as my date. In April she broke up with me, ironically, via text message."

"Hopefully not while driving," Mimi quipped.

"To be honest, I wasn't aware we were officially dating. I didn't think we were serious enough to 'break up.'"

"But you were serious enough to sleep with her."

"Were you sleeping with Gerard?"

They watched each other in a silent standoff before Mimi looked away. "I guess it's hard to find the person you want to spend forever with."

Hard to find them, or hard to hold on to them?

She laid her head back onto her hand. A few beats passed while he listened to her breathe, feeling protective of her—responsible for her.

"If my reelection campaign takes a turn and the spotlight finds you..." With the arm already wrapped around her, he gave her a gentle squeeze. "I won't let it touch you."

"You can't promise that."

"I can promise if it does touch you, I'll do everything in my power to extract you from the conversation. You don't deserve any of this. Hell, that was the main reason..." He fell silent, opting not to finish the thought he'd started.

"That was the main reason for what?" She lifted her head, the dent between her eyebrows warning him to tell her the truth or face her wrath.

"Like back then, I'd never ask you to be a part of my world now. To sacrifice what you believe in, what you love, to stand at the side of a man who's an oil tycoon first and a politician second." He let out a dry chuckle. "That must sound like your worst nightmare."

Correction: that wasn't irritation on her face. Mimi was *pissed*.

"First off, Chase Ferguson—" she punctuated each word by stabbing his breastbone while her eyes drilled into him "—you are a man with a heart and soul. A *good* man, your choice in women notwithstanding." A dig he let her have since she was right. Women always wanted something he wasn't willing to give, or were only there for the arm candy he provided. While he found neither of those situations objectionable, they didn't add up to a very flattering relationship record.

"Secondly," she continued, not through defending his honor, "you're a businessman and a politician. A damn good one if what I uncovered online can be believed."

"Uncovered? What did you uncover?"

Her face pinked as her gaze bounced around the room—landing everywhere but on him. He'd bet his bank account she hadn't meant to say that last part. He physically turned her chin and forced her guilty, dark eyes back on him.

"Mimi Andrix, did you *Google* me?"

"When I received that letter out of the blue—that *impersonal* letter—I was curious. I vowed not to go further than the city's website, but I clicked through a few of those search pages and..."

Her cheeks burned red.

"And?" He prompted.

She licked her lips before admitting, "I found an interesting website."

The heat of embarrassment burned Miriam's face. Admitting she'd dug up information on Chase like a besotted highschooler was humiliating.

"A website about me?" he asked, clearly bemused.

"Yes."

"What was on it?" He mashed a decorative pillow under his neck to hold his head up so he could properly interrogate her. "Were there photos?"

"*Yes*, egomaniac. And...stories."

"Stories?" One eyebrow arched high on his forehead.

"Fictional ones." She covered her eyes with one

hand. "They were so bad. The worst fan fiction ever. About how she dreamed of you and her…" She moved her hand to gesture. "Together."

A rough rumble of laughter shook his chest, jostling her. She opened one eye to find him still laughing, throat bobbing, and was that…yes, she believed it was. She swiped a tear from the corner of his eye. He'd laughed himself to tears.

"That's…" He swiped his own eyes and sniffed. "I don't know what that is. Damn funny."

He was so appealing when he was this relaxed.

"At first I thought maybe she was a jilted ex-girlfriend, but then it was clear she'd never met you."

"What tipped you off?" He grinned, loving every second of this.

"She brought up having sex with you on a horse and—"

That brought forth another crack of laughter as fresh tears sprang to his eyes. She laughed with him, the hardy, happy sound as infectious as he was. He recovered quickly, rolling toward the back of the couch and wedging her between the leather and his hard, warm body.

"How do you know that isn't true?" His tone was sober, his eyes narrowed and assessing.

"Other than you don't seem the type to attempt sex on a horse," she said with a small giggle. "The day I invited you horseback riding."

His gaze swept to one side. "How come I don't remember that?"

"I asked if you wanted to go riding and you said you didn't trust a beast that large with your bodily safety. It stood out in my mind because you were from

Texas. I thought all Texans were brought up riding horses."

"I remember that conversation now. Horses are smart. I imagine they don't always like to be ridden. And once I'm up there, there's only one way to go."

"Down." She ran a fingertip along his bristled jawline. "They are smart animals."

"On that we agree. Horses are very smart and deserve our respect."

"So, we're on the same side of the fence on one more topic," she whispered against his lips. He was close enough to kiss, his delicious weight pressing her deeper into the couch's cushions. "Does that bring our grand total to three?"

"I can think of one more." He took her lips hostage, making out with her long and slow. One hand gripped her hip before sliding under her shirt to tickle her bare skin.

Her mind melted, her body doing a good job of following suit, as he made love to her mouth with his. He wasn't wrong. Sex was another topic both their bodies and minds agreed on.

They'd always been physically compatible. They'd proven it time and time again during many summer nights past and they were proving it again in the winter wonderland of his massive mansion. Earlier he'd claimed her against the wall. Now he seemed bent on *reclaiming* her.

She couldn't think of a single reason to argue.

"This is *incredible*." Miriam lounged in the hot tub, bubbling water tickling her bare breasts and liquefying her sore muscles.

Chase had done a good job of liquefying them earlier today—a few times.

He sat on the other side of the round tub—in-ground
like the pool—and let out a long, gruff hum. A hum
of satisfaction and relaxation. She liked being with
him—yes for the sex, which was amazing but also for
the moments that followed. She hadn't been apart from
him for more than a handful of minutes today and she
didn't care to leave his side until she officially walked
out of this mansion.

Crazy? Possibly. But she could handle a brief affair with him. She was no longer a carefree twenty-
three-year-old whose life had been overwhelmed by
the sexy city boy from Texas. She was a grown, independent, responsible woman with people who counted
on her—both professionally and personally. She was
old enough and wise enough to understand that what
had kept them apart years ago was alive and well.
Their interests were as different as a Dallas oil field
and a Montana nature preserve.

If, say, they had a shot at coupledom—an insane
thought, but she allowed herself to have it—it'd mean
her moving to Dallas and leaving her family and her
beloved job behind *or* Chase moving to Montana
where he'd…what? Run for mayor here? Take a seat
on the county board? Fall back on his law degree and
hang a shingle in town?

It was preposterous, the idea that Chase the famous
mayor and oil tycoon would move away from his beloved state to live in the wilderness.

They were doomed.

Which made things easier. Back when they were together she hadn't known they were doomed. Or rather,

she'd been the *last* to know. Knowing up front meant no castle-building on the clouds. She could enjoy what they had at face value and walk away with some really great memories.

"It is incredible." His agreement interrupted her deep thoughts and she opened her eyes to find his closed, his head resting back, arms spread out and resting on the edge of the hot tub.

She saw no need to share her thoughts with him. With anyone other than herself. And that certainty—along with knowing they were doomed—also felt really, really good.

She would let any thoughts of what happened next between them rise and swirl and disappear like steam from the hot tub. But she wouldn't deny herself the treasure of being with him while they were stranded.

Later, when Chase took her hand, she allowed him to lead her upstairs and into his bedroom.

Sixteen

The following day was nothing like the one that preceded it. Rather than dance around each other and spend most of the day naked, they bundled up and headed outside.

The snow was barely falling now, and Miriam had spotted a snowplow making slow progress through one of the neighborhoods at the base of the hill. They were still under several feet of snow, and the temperature remained stubbornly frigid, but at least the snow had stopped. People were starting to emerge from their homes, and from the vantage point of the upstairs library this morning she'd spotted a few brightly colored parkas dotting the whitewashed landscape.

"Ready?" Chase positioned the round plastic disc on a hill at the side of the house and held it steady for her to climb on.

"You first," she said, tipping her chin.

"No, thanks." He twisted the toboggan deeper into the snow.

"Chicken."

"Sticks and stones, Mimi. Get your very fine rear on this sled."

"It's a toboggan."

"Stop delaying." His dark hair ruffled in the breeze, his ears bright red. He'd torn his hat off a few minutes ago when he'd gone searching for the toboggan, or *sled* as he called it, complaining he was hot. Only Chase Ferguson could be hot in fifteen-degree weather.

"After shoveling, you deserve to have some fun. Maybe we should go down together."

His eyes were uncooperative slits, but he surprisingly agreed. "Okay, fine. Take hold of this while I put my hat back on."

She squealed her way to the bottom of the hill, nestled against his front while he sat behind her. When they came to a landing at a cluster of trees she was glad they hadn't mowed into, she'd collected a pile of snow between her legs.

"Again?" Warm lips touched her cheek. "Or do you want to go inside and warm up?"

"Again!" She couldn't help herself. She hadn't done this in years. This was too fun not to continue.

They went again, *and again*, until her legs were jelly from climbing the hill and Chase had flat out given up. He lied and said he was making snow angels, but she could tell he was taking a beat to catch his breath. After their final climb up the hill, he leaned the toboggan against the garage and they shut out the cold, peeling off their snow-packed outfits before dashing inside to start a fire.

Once they were dressed in comfy clothes, fire lit and mugs of soup for both of them, Miriam's nose finally began to thaw.

"Told you I'd make a mountain man out of you yet."

"You're very persuasive." Chase finished his mug of soup and set it aside, scrubbing his hands down his legs and then holding his palms in front of the fire. "I miss Texas. Shoveling is for the birds."

"I'm sure if you lived here you'd be able to find someone to shovel for you." When he looked over at her, his brow a contemplative mar, she said, "I mean if you visit here again. In the winter. It doesn't always snow this much."

She pressed her lips together to stop the spillway of words.

"Speaking of, I need to find someone to do just that," he said. "The city will take care of the street, but this long driveway is too much work for one shovel."

"I have snow-removal guys on speed dial for my job. I can call one later on today."

"Or tomorrow." He locked his eyes on hers. "No sense in beating the street plow."

"Right."

They fell silent, listening to the fire snap and pop. Her time here was ending. She'd only been here a few days, but it felt longer. Like that summer past had bled into a fall she'd forgotten and a winter that lingered.

The same niggling, disturbing sensation of no time having passed occurred while she and Chase loaded the dishwasher. He rinsed her mug and took the spoon from her hand while she'd dropped in the detergent pod. He shut the device and pressed Start, and just like that, they'd perfected the dance in the kitchen without a word.

Like a couple who knew each other.

Like a couple who hadn't been apart for ten years.

In his room that night, she opted to leave her yoga pants and T-shirt on, though she did lose the sweatshirt. When she climbed beneath the covers, however, he snatched the blankets off her.

"What's this?" He gestured to her wardrobe.

"I'm cold!"

"You won't be with me next to you." He gestured to himself. "Human heater."

"By your own admission, you spent most of this year *not* sleeping next to a naked woman—" she sat up and gathered the blankets over her body "—wouldn't want to spoil you unnecessarily."

"Low blow, Andrix." He tugged off his sweatshirt and dropped his jeans and she pulled the blankets to her nose and admired his rock-hard, sculpted, beautiful body.

He tossed his clothes over a chair and she found it cute. From the outside, he appeared to be a neat freak yet he never truly made his bed and always tossed his clothes instead of folding or hanging them. It made him somehow more approachable. More relatable.

On her side, he lifted the blankets. "Scoot."

"This is my side!" she argued but scooted.

"Excuse me. This is my bed, *interloper*. Do as I say."

Once under the covers, he looped one arm around

her waist and shoved the other beneath his pillow. On his side, he faced her, his eyes heavy.

They'd had afternoon sex in her room today. After they'd eaten lunch and warmed up from playing in the snow, he'd come in and grasped her hips, grinding into her from behind. She'd gladly stopped what she was doing—packing—and made love to him.

Made love.

She thought the words with an eye roll, but there wasn't a better way to phrase it.

He'd always had an intimate way about him that was impossible to deny. Temporary or not, when they were together, they were both focused on the finite. The immediate moment—the breaths they shared. The noises they made. The sensations in their bodies turning them inside out.

She hated to admit it, but she was hoping they'd have another go at it tonight.

"You're too tired," she said, but noticed her own eyelids weighing heavy.

"Too tired for what?" But he knew. He grabbed a handful of her T-shirt. "You're the one who's dressed. I took that as a lack of interest."

"Where you're concerned, Mr. Mayor, there's never been lack of interest." She'd meant the comment to tease, but her voice came out husky.

"I'm never too tired." His hand warmed her belly and coasted north until he found her bare breast. He tweaked a nipple and she squirmed. He did it again and he smiled. "I feel a second wind coming on."

Her answer was a lust-heavy exhale.

The blankets were gone in a sudden *whoosh* and

his eyes went from half-lidded haze to heated gaze in a split second.

"Off." He plucked her T-shirt. "I'll wrestle with these stretchy prison bars," he said of her tight pants. He made short work of them, throwing her socks over his shoulder as she tore off her T-shirt. He lost the boxer briefs next and lay against her body, every simmering inch of hard muscle warming wherever he touched.

"Still cold?"

She shivered but shook her head. That shiver had nothing to do with cold and everything to do with the anticipation of his clever mouth. His attentive hands. His—

Chase's tongue circled her nipple and his fingers spread her legs. He dipped his middle finger into her well of desire, finding her wet and ready.

"No, I don't believe you're cold any longer." With a wicked grin, he kissed his way down her body and positioned himself between her legs. He stayed down there a long time, not coming up for air even when she begged him not to make her come again. Instead he wrung one more out of her, one that sent her fluttering pulse into overdrive. Her shouts of completion echoed off his bedroom walls and rang off the wide windows overlooking the silent, snowy lake.

She didn't know how long she lay on her side, suffering aftershocks from back-to-back powerful releases. When she finally heard his voice it was through a head stuffed with cotton.

"Sleep, beautiful girl," he whispered into her ear. "You earned it."

A soft but firm kiss hit the corner of her mouth and

She meant to turn over and relay her appreciation, but instead slipped into the gauzy realm of deep sleep and dreamed of nothing at all.

Chase woke up confused about what time it was. The moon was out and reflecting on the snow, making it appear like early morning, but the sky was pitch-black, stars dotting the nighttime canvas.

He checked his phone for the time—3:00 a.m.—and then rolled over to wrap a palm around Mimi's breast.

Neither she nor her breasts were there.

He lay on his back in the semidark listening for her. She hadn't gone far. From the sound of fluttering pages coming from the room outside his, she was flipping through a book. After taking her on his tongue, he'd been sure she'd sleep through the night. He was beat from shoveling, sledding—or *tobogganing*—and honest-to-goodness fatigue had had him drifting off in a matter of minutes. Short-lived, evidently. Whatever had woken him, be it Mimi's wandering about or a dream that had already lost its potency after jarring him awake, he was too alert to fall asleep again.

Climbing out of bed, he was greeted by frigid air in the room. He grabbed his phone to check the app for his thermostat, bumping it up a few degrees. Then he checked his stocks out of habit, narrowly avoided his email and left the device on his nightstand. At the door of his bedroom, he found her where he'd imagined.

Wrapped in a thick quilt in the library and curled on the armchair facing the window over the lake. She was flipping through one of the books from the shelves. A murder mystery by the looks of it.

"Fan of Patterson?"

She looked up, briefly startled by him standing there. "Who isn't?"

"Good point."

She slid her gaze down his boxers-only attire. "Put some clothes on. It's cold."

"Share your blanket instead." He tugged a corner of it, exposing her bare legs. She had on panties and a T-shirt, but nothing else. Perfect.

"This chair isn't big enough for—Hey!" Her exclaimed argument faded into soft laughter as the hardbound book hit the floor with a *thunk*. He lifted her and set her on his lap, cradling her close and wrapping that blanket around his legs while he was at it.

"Plenty of room," he said of their shared seat. "What are you doing up?"

"Couldn't sleep." This close, he could see the feathered soft lines at the corners of her eyes, the faint smile lines around her mouth. The freckles that had been out in droves years ago were fainter but still present, likely from her work outdoors.

"I did everything in my power to put you out for an entire night. I was hoping you'd sleep in."

"Why? Were you going to deliver me an avocado-and-protein smoothie in bed?"

He captured her hand in his and wove their fingers together, admiring the way her long, elegant fingers fit against his tanner, wider ones.

"I was going to make pancakes."

"You're lying."

"Tomorrow, or today technically," he corrected, "is looking like our last day together. I assume once the driveway is cleared you'll go home."

"What will you do?" she asked instead of addressing his comment.

"I don't know." He pulled in a breath and let it out. "Stay. Leave. Depends."

She examined their linked hands and said nothing.

"Mimi." That brought her dark eyes to his. He took in her pretty, delicate features in the streaming moonlight, weighed her hand in his and absolutely did not say what he was thinking. Which was that his staying or leaving had everything to do with her.

He'd come here to get away. And yes, in a distant part of his mind he'd considered that he might run into her while he was here. He'd considered dropping in on her at work and buying her a coffee under the guise of discussing the photo and the letter sent from his office. He'd wanted to see her. See if she was all right. Find out if she hated him for what he did, or if they'd outgrown what had been between them.

He'd have died before admitting the unfinished business, but after he'd run into her at the supermarket he'd concluded that was exactly what it was. When she'd called to invite him to her family's house, he'd declined, guessing he'd be unwelcomed by her family and knowing that Mimi couldn't help being kind.

He never expected her to drive out to see him, end up trapped with him in this snowstorm. And even though he'd been determined to have her in his arms once she was stuck here with him, he never imagined it would be this easy. This satisfying. This…right. He hadn't counted on the onslaught of powerful emotions from years ago to resurface, either. Feelings for her he hadn't examined and would prefer not to, but stood before him now like an immovable wall.

He could see now how much she'd mattered to him back then. He'd concluded that the cure was time and space; distance should have erased the intensity between them. He'd assumed the bond they'd had then had been broken. It was beginning to appear as if it'd been merely…interrupted.

Hell, maybe he should tell her what was on his mind. He had no idea what was going on in her head and guessing would do him no good… Maybe he'd been wrong assuming she wouldn't fit into his world. Maybe—

"I think you should stay," she said, all but stealing his next breath.

"You do?" he asked like an imbecile.

"Yes. Bigfork is beautiful in the winter and you haven't been here for very long. Once they clear the snow, they'll cordon off part of the lake for ice skating. Especially if the weather stays this cold." She chattered another couple of seconds like a tour guide listing the many amenities that could occupy his time while he was in Bigfork.

But she failed to list herself among them.

"What about you?"

"Well, I live here." She looped her arms around his neck and placed a quick kiss on his lips. "I don't need to see the sights."

"I mean what are you doing while I'm here?"

She shrugged casually. "Working, most likely. I only took off through Monday."

He frowned. "Mimi."

"What?"

"Can I…" He was out of his element, which was frustrating. He never hesitated to ask for what he wanted. And what he wanted was the attention of the woman on his lap for a few more days. Hell, weeks. He didn't know. Just…more. He pulled in a breath and blew out a gruff invitation, "Do you want to grab dinner some night while I'm here, or not?"

"Charming." But she smiled when she said it.

"Sorry. I'm…tired."

"Well…" She offered a careless shrug like he wasn't hanging on her every syllable. "I might have a free night next week. You have my number."

It was a blowoff if he'd ever heard one. And he'd delivered a few in his day.

She kissed him, lingering at his bottom lip to give it a gentle bite. "I don't want to think about work. I want to think about…" She reached between his legs. "Right now."

He let out a grunt and she crushed his lips with a kiss while her hand kept stroking. There'd been a brief objection in his brain but damn if he could access it now. Her touching him had erased any brewing argument—sound or not. He was vaguely aware he should be stopping her to continue this discussion and put it to rest for good, but another stroke and her moaned "I want you" against his lips successfully deterred him.

He unwound the piled blanket from her body and shifted her on his lap. Her lips never left his. He had her divested of the white cotton panties in a blink. She yanked down his boxer briefs as far as his thighs and positioned herself over his heavy erection.

Sweat beaded his brow. He cupped her nape with one hand and rested his forehead on hers.

"Wait." His voice came out on a harsh breath. "Condom. Or…not…"

She froze. The whites of her eyes were bright in the moonlight streaming in behind him. She gulped and that was the moment he knew they were on the same page. Despite her flippant reaction to his asking her out, Mimi was invested. In him. At least for the moment.

He brushed her hair over her shoulder. "We can move this to the bedroom, or we can stay here and have nothing between us." It was a risk, and more than a physical one. "Tell me it's possible."

"Do you mean am I on the pill? Am I clean?" She pressed a finger to his bottom lip. "Yes to both, but..."

"Too much?" he guessed. No barrier put them back where they were ten years ago. In her cramped twin bed where nothing—not even a thin coat of rubber—had stood between them.

"I loved how you felt. Just you. Just us." And more than anything, he needed that connection now. For reasons he couldn't explain—or maybe reasons he wouldn't admit.

His heart gave a dangerous lurch forward.

"Are you... A lot has happened since then," she said.

"Not as much as you think." He pressed a soft kiss to her lips and cradled the back of her head, her hair's silken strands tickling his forearm. "The last woman I slept with without a condom was you."

He felt more than saw her pull her head back.

"For old time's sake?" she asked, her smile nervous rather than sly. It was more than that and she knew it, but in this dim, moonlit space on their last night together, he'd give her the out.

"For old time's sake," he agreed.

Straddling him, she held his gaze captive and sank down so slowly he had to weld his back teeth together to keep from coming too soon. She emitted a familiar sigh of pleasure that he echoed. She was soft and warm—everything he remembered mixed with everything he now knew. Being with her was different, but also the same.

She still absolutely *undid* him.

He tilted his hips, sinking into her and emitting a harsh exhale. He guided himself deep, noticing when she trembled against him. She was heat and silk and wet. Beauty and kindness and giving. Always so damn giving. Making this last would take a feat of superhuman willpower, but he'd make it last for her.

Her head was thrown back, her nipples pressing the thin white T-shirt. He absorbed her gasps, closing his lips over hers, marking her lust-heavy gaze in his memory. He made love to her with reverence, far from through with her, and hoped his actions conveyed what he hadn't been able to say. That there was a reason for her to say yes to dinner, to say yes to *him* while he was here.

No. *Longer.*

Their lazy thrusts gained speed and it was that feverish pace that brought her to orgasm. She tensed and clutched him deep, coming with his name on her lips. He followed, spilling inside her and branding her his.

Whether she knew it or not.

Seventeen

Chase was in the shower when the gate's call button rang. Miriam sent a glance up the staircase and dashed for the door, wondering if she should answer it. Who was up here in the middle of a blizzard?

She depressed the button labeled Speaker and hoped that was the right one. "Yes?"

"Good morning, ma'am. My partner and I are plowing driveways and I noticed yours needs clearing," came a slightly southern accent. She backed away from the box and studied the video screen. The black-and-white picture showed a man in the cab of a pickup truck, a woman in a scarf and ballcap in the seat next to him. His face was pleasant, his goatee neatly trimmed. Young. She guessed him a twenty-something. She had a soft spot for hardworking twentysomethings. "The main road's done," he said with a glance in his rearview mirror. "We can have you cleared in thirty minutes tops."

She remembered her own climb up the driveway. His must've been treacherous.

"How'd you climb the hill to the gate?"

A slightly chagrined smile decorated his handsome features. "Cleared free of charge, ma'am. We're taking the chance you'll hire us to finish."

Well. She couldn't say no to that. She'd planned on giving Chase her friend Rodney's number to call about removing the snow, but these two were already here. Who knew if Rodney was even available? She couldn't turn away budding entrepreneurs.

After a brief discussion of price, she agreed and buzzed them in. Feeling proud for handling it by herself, she called upstairs. "Snowplow guy's here!"

It was a safe guess that her voice hadn't carried all the way to his bedroom. This house was enormous. He needed one of those damn speaker boxes for each *floor*.

She made a fresh pot of coffee, intending to take some out to the two working in the driveway, but a knock at the door interrupted her task.

"That was fast," she said to herself, encountering Chase at the bottom of the stairs.

"What was fast?" His hair was damp, and he was dressed in a sweater and jeans. He looked so good she was struck dumb for a beat. "Did I hear a knock?"

"Lucky for you, I was here to answer your gate. We are being shoveled out as we speak." She climbed to her toes, taking a handful of his cable-knit sweater and kissing his firm mouth. *Mmm.* He always smelled good. "I negotiated a fair price."

She walked for the front door, Chase on her heels. "How'd he get to the gate?"

"Don't be alarmed, Mr. Mayor, I asked that, too. He cleared it in the hopes we'd say yes to his offer."

"Mimi, wait."

But she'd already yanked open the door. There she found the pair of entrepreneurs, the goateed guy holding a video camera and the blonde aiming her cell phone. The sound of electronic shutter snaps told her that the other woman was taking pictures. Questions from both of them came flying at her.

"Miriam Andrix, is it true that you and Chase Ferguson are rekindling your romance?"

"How do you plan to make it work being on opposite sides of the oil debate?"

"Mr. Mayor, are you planning on moving to Bigfork permanently or will Miriam be relocating to Dallas?"

Chase grabbed Miriam's arm, tugging her roughly behind him. To the pair spouting questions, he growled, "Get the hell off my property or I'm calling the authorities."

The snowplowers-slash-reporters...or whatever they were made one last attempt, shouting, "Chase, are you and Miriam in love? Will you be planning a wedding here in Montana?" before Chase shut the door with a slam. Snow swirled in from the porch and gathered in the entrance. He turned and melted Mimi's skin off with a laser-hot glare.

"I didn't know..." she started, but her voice trailed off.

"I know."

He pulled his phone from his pocket and opened the door, shutting himself outside. She listened at the door as more machine-gun-fire questions sliced the air, but one voice was louder than the others—Chase's. He was addressing someone on the phone, the police if Miriam had to guess, and saying that two unwanted guests had trespassed on his property. She watched out the window as the fakers scampered to the truck and backed down the driveway.

Chase came back inside, his damp hair dusted with snow that had frozen into icicles. He punched the Gate Closed button.

"What was that?" she asked. That insanity had happened right in front of her, yet she still couldn't make sense of it.

"That," he said as he pocketed his phone, "was your official welcome to my opponent's political campaign."

Phone to his ear, Chase waited impatiently through two, then three rings. Halfway through the third, Emmett picked up.

"What the hell is going on?" Chase barked into the phone.

Emmett's voice went as rigid as rebar. "What happened?"

"Two spies or journalists talked their way past Mimi and into my front yard. They snapped several pictures of us."

"Wearing what?" Emmett asked. Smartly.

"Clothes. We weren't doing anything." *At the time.*

"What's Mimi doing there?" Emmett's question was more to gather intel than pass judgement.

"She was dropping off pie when the weather snowed her in." And that was all the detail his friend was getting. "Care to explain why I'm fighting off paparazzi at my vacation home?"

"A blog posted early this morning. I literally read it five minutes ago. Haven't had a chance to think through the implications let alone call to alert you."

"In the same vein as the letter that arrived with the photo?"

"I don't know. It's gone."

"What do you mean it's gone?"

"The letter and the photo. I assume you didn't throw it out?"

Emmett knew him—knew he wouldn't throw away a photo of Mimi even if it was a photo where she was protesting the very industry that he upheld. "I locked it in the lap drawer of my desk."

A sniff that might mean *could've guessed* came through the phone.

"What gives with the Bigfork welcome? Opportunists?" Chase asked.

"Too soon. The only way someone could've tracked you down was if they already knew you were there. Who knows Mimi is there?"

"Her sister." But he doubted Kris was their culprit. She and Mimi were close. "I have no idea what Kristine would gain by ratting out Mimi."

"Lucky find, probably," Em concluded. "They were after a reaction from you and got a twofer when she opened the door."

"Send me the link to the blog, will you?"

"Will do. I'll question the staff. If the leak's not on Mimi's end, it has to be on ours. Enjoy the rest of your vacation, boss." Then he was gone.

Chase expected to find Mimi wringing her hands

after hearing his side of the conversation. Instead, she stood with her arms folded awaiting explanation.

"I promised I would shield you from any backlash, and that's what I intend to do," he told her. "In the meantime, this changes things. I suggest you stay put rather than—"

"This doesn't change anything. I'm not staying here. I *can't* stay here. I don't live here. I have to work."

"Mimi—"

"I can handle myself, Chase." She unfolded her arms and let them dangle at her sides, looking suddenly tired. "I've been handling myself without your help for a long time. You don't have to be a white knight."

"I'm not trying to be a white knight," he snapped. She didn't know the world of politics. They wouldn't give up until they found the dirt they were looking for. "They're going to harass you, and then harass your family."

"You said you would handle it. Handle it. I am *not* hiding and waiting for them to go away before I resume my life. What's the point in my hiding here?"

Because I want you here.

"I can protect you here," he said instead. "Provided you don't buzz in anyone else through that gate."

"I'm sorry I fell for the oldest trick in the book." Her eyes flicked to one side before meeting his. "I should've asked you first."

He wrapped his hands around her small shoulders, consoling her. "Right, the old pretend-to-be-snow-removal-guys-to-capture-photos-of-the-mayor-with-his-old-flame trick."

That brought a soft smile to her face.

"They play dirty."

"I've never minded getting dirty." She tipped her chin and pegged him with admirable ferocity. Once upon a time, she'd been his and he'd let her go, believing she couldn't handle his life.

Had he been right and she'd grown stronger because of it? Or had he been wrong and this strength had been there all along?

He knew the answer. It wasn't a pretty one.

"Sit tight for a few hours. I'll find out what's going on." His phone buzzed and he glanced at the screen to find the link to the blog post. "Do me that favor?"

She nodded her agreement and walked to the kitchen for a cup of coffee.

Chase began reading.

Emmett's gruff voice bounced off the walls of Chase's Dallas home and Stef paused in the doorway, wiggling her key from the lock. She'd come over to borrow a staple gun since Zach was out of town and she didn't have a key to his house. Chase had given her a key a long time ago. One she'd never bothered returning.

But she hadn't expected to find Emmett here. He was crowding her space an awful lot lately. She would have suspected he'd followed her here if she hadn't arrived second.

His phone conversation was brief, and she guessed he was talking to Chase about something serious given his clipped tone and the mention of Mimi. There was a name she hadn't heard in a while. She peeked into the dining room to find Emmett, his broad back covered in a white button-down shirt, his very short hair close cut in the shape of his perfect head.

He was a big, muscly, glaring guy. Stefanie preferred guys fun, easygoing and quick to smile. Lean muscle, not bulk. Kind eyes rather than Emmett's intense stony stare. She supposed those attributes made him perfect for security. And besides, it didn't matter that he wasn't her type. They hated each other. It was a silently agreed upon fact. It was sort of magical, actually, how they were each peeved merely by the other's existence.

"That sounded serious," she said, announcing herself.

He turned and glared and said nothing.

Typical.

"Anything I can help with?" She grinned, knowing his answer.

"Did you write an article about your brother having an affair with a woman who vehemently protests the oil industry?"

"No."

"Then you can't help." He slid the phone into his pocket and grabbed his coat from the back of a chair.

"What did the article say?"

He didn't so much as slow down as he blew past her. The disturbingly manly scent of his leather coat tickled her nostrils.

"Emmett? Is everything okay?" she called after him.

At the door, he paused, letting the cool November air blow in.

"It's clearly public knowledge. I can tell by your gruffer-than-usual attitude," she added.

He let out a long-suffering sigh—a reaction she'd come to expect. She assumed it was also a sigh of surrender, but no confession followed.

"Lock up," were the only words he spoke before stepping outside.

"Emmett!" But he was done gracing her with his presence. Gruff, grouchy, impossible. What did her brother see in that guy?

She huffed before shutting the door behind him. Let Em and her brother deal with their mayoral drama. Why should she care?

She went back to searching for the staple gun, irritated that on a need-to-know basis she was the *last* to know.

Well. She had important things to do, too. Like decorate for her favorite holiday. Her brothers used to help her string the lights in her bedroom when they lived at home, but now they were too busy to help. Her apartment remained sadly unadorned. With Chase in Montana, Zach in Chicago and her father in the middle of the ocean, she'd been left no choice but to fend for herself.

"You could've asked Emmett," she said with a sarcastic chuckle as she checked another drawer in the tool chest. And wouldn't he *love* that? Coming to the aid of the lesser Ferguson… He was as full of Christmas cheer as the Mojave Desert was water.

She could hang her own damn Christmas lights.

She shut the last of the drawers, propping her fists on her hips in frustration before tipping her head and spotting the staple gun hanging on a hook on the black pegboard between two cabinets. "Gotcha."

The small victory's glory faded as she walked for

the front door. Neither Chase nor Emmett trusted her and she didn't like that. What if she could help?

Behind the wheel of her white sports car, she punched a button to close the gate behind her and pointed in the direction of Chase's office. She'd served a summer internship there a few years ago, and guess who had entrusted her with the key?

Another key she'd never given up.

Whether it was curiosity or hurt feelings driving her actions, she didn't know. It didn't matter. She was a *doer*. She wasn't going to stay in the dark no matter what Emmett said. Chase was *her* brother, after all.

Eighteen

"I handled it for real this time." Miriam waggled her cell phone before relinquishing it to the kitchen island, feeling a touch of residual guilt.

She kept thinking and rethinking about the reporters at the gate earlier this morning. She should have known. Of course, there was no way she *could* have known. Chase held her blameless, but it didn't keep her from reliving the moment she'd pressed that button and wishing she hadn't.

Chase, finished grilling ham-and-cheese sandwiches, slid them onto two waiting plates. The sight of melted cheese made her mouth water. He stirred the pot of tomato soup on the stove.

"These must be your specialty," she said of the perfectly golden wedges.

"They are." He sent her a wink over his shoulder and went back to stirring the soup.

"I know Rodney personally. He will plow your driveway without snapping a single photo."

"Do you like crackers in your tomato soup?"

"I'll dip my sandwich in it instead."

"Exactly the way I like it. Another topic of agreement."

Yes. They'd found several.

"He'll be here within the hour," she said rather than think of one *particular* act they had in common and were really freaking good at doing. "If you want me to handle that transaction, I can wait to take my shower until later."

"I have it." He ladled the soup into bowls, and lifted his eyes to hers. "Stop beating yourself up."

"I'm not beating myself up," she argued, though she kind of was.

"You're not worrying about me? Concerned that my campaign has been undone by a headstrong woman who protests the oil industry?"

Okay, a little. She couldn't help it. "*Protested*, past tense. I don't protest any longer."

"We suspected backlash could come as a result of the photograph. Emmett had a plan in place if it went live. He just hadn't expected scouts to find us here. And he hadn't counted on you being here, either."

"You wouldn't have let them through the gate, would you?"

"I've been doing this a long time, Mimi."

Which meant his answer was no, he wouldn't have.

"Do you trust Emmett?"

"With every detail of my professional—and personal—life."

That made her feel marginally better. Chase had someone else looking out for him—someone he could trust implicitly. She knew his family was loyal to him and he to them, but she also knew how nice it was to have that one person you could talk to in shorthand. Kris was that person for her.

"How do you stand it?" She dragged her spoon through her bowl of bright red soup. "Having people excited to expose your secrets like that?"

"I ignore it. It's a small price to pay to do the work I do. Besides, I don't have any skeletons in my closet." He gave her another teasing wink. "Save you."

"Ha-ha."

"It's not worth giving my time or attention. Not worth yours, either. There are a lot of people who don't have anything better to do than yell about what's going on in the world. The problem is, they yell and don't actually do anything. So while they're yelling, I aim to be the one doing. The one doing makes the most progress."

Spoon in hand, she paused to let that soak in. He sat next to her, eating his lunch, probably not thinking about the words that had exited his mouth. About how profound and meaningful they were. When she first met him, she'd been as mesmerized by the way he talked as she was by the way he looked. She'd been fascinated by his passionate and clear statements. Moved by his confidence. He was someone people loved to follow. A true leader.

His city needed him. Now that she'd shut down her selfish need for payback—or whatever the hell she'd been doing—she saw how *good* he was. Her instincts were spot-on. He was rich and powerful, but his will wouldn't be bent by the promise of becoming richer or more powerful.

"You're good for Dallas," she concluded.

He turned his head and watched her for a beat. "Thank you. I don't often care what other people think. But your opinion has always mattered. Always." He grabbed her hand and gave her fingers a gentle squeeze. "I know you mean it. Not many people say what they mean."

Wasn't that the truth? Her job required a modicum of political know-how in the environmental circle and hardly anyone said what they meant. She thought of her proclivity to speak her mind rather than be careful. And thought with a smile about how she'd make a horrible mayor's wife.

Wife?

She dropped her spoon with a clang. Where the hell had that thought come from?

"You okay?" The mayor of Dallas crunched into his sandwich, concern darkening his eyes.

"Yeah. Yes. Fine." Oh sure, she sounded totally fine. The mayor's *wife*. She hadn't had a thought like that since…

Since he'd worn nothing but her cheap bedsheets in her ratty apartment. Since he'd been standing in her kitchen making a lunch not dissimilar to this one. It might have been ham and cheese with potato chips, and they'd dined on her tiny twin bed and ate off paper plates, but this *felt* the same.

Or do you feel the same?

The sandwiches were gourmet and the plates were

breakable this time around but there was a lot about Chase that hadn't changed. A lot about her that hadn't changed. Like the fact that she still wanted a family and a husband. She wanted an adventure, and a life beyond success at work. She'd imagined a man would fill that role eventually, but she hadn't been looking. And for some reason, sitting here with Chase now made her wonder if she hadn't been looking because she knew what she wanted couldn't be found *here*.

Because he'd always been in Dallas.

The days they'd spent together had snapped seamlessly against the days back when she'd first fallen in love with him. As fast as those days seemed to pass by that summer, being here with him was like being frozen in time. Like they'd been trapped inside a snow globe and given a second chance.

Her stomach flipped, her mind along with it. She couldn't act on those feelings—not a single one of them. She'd made that decision the moment she let him slip her out of her clothes. The moment she'd allowed him to make love to her, she'd promised herself she couldn't and wouldn't allow him access to her heart.

Not again.

"Excuse me." She practically ran from the kitchen to her bedroom, shoving ideas about time-freezing snow globes out of her head. This affair was completely separate from their past—not an extension of it. No matter how much it seemed that the present had fractured and allowed the past to seep in, it hadn't. Remembering moments with him was normal, and definitely not a sign that they could've been more or still could be more.

She lifted her half-full suitcase onto the bed and began packing the rest of her clothes and shoes into it. Her mind volleyed arguments that she was overreacting, but her heart was too tender to spend another moment in this house—or with this man. She rerouted her thoughts on work. Her to-do list waiting for her tomorrow morning. She needed to return to normalcy. To pop this bubble that bent reality and made it seem as though Chase and she belonged together. In reality, and outside of this snowstorm, he lived in Dallas and she lived here. He worked in politics, and she fought for funds from state heads. Once she returned to her own reasonably sized apartment, had a semblance of *normal* after three fantastic, but abnormal, days, everything would go back to the way it should be.

"Was it something I said?" Chase hovered in the doorway.

"Rodney will be here to clear the driveway soon." She unfolded a shirt and rolled it instead, shoving it into the corner of her suitcase.

"Yes, but there's no rush."

"I know." But even that sounded defensive.

He stepped deeper into the room, knocking her equilibrium for a loop. "Was the soup bad?"

She shot him a quick warning glare. She didn't want to joke around right now. She didn't want to *like him* right now. But she did. She did like him, dammit. She liked the way he took care of her, the way he kissed her and the way he'd followed her in here to make sure she was okay.

Which was exactly why she needed to leave.

"I'll finish lunch. I just… I want to get this done. Maybe grab a shower before I go."

He came closer, his breath in her ear when he gripped her hips from behind. The move reminded her of the other night, when he'd followed that move with a kiss, his fists squeezing her flesh possessively.

"I can join you if you like," he said, his voice gruff.

"No." She couldn't allow more blurred lines. "It's better if I go. Let's call that last bout on the library chair the end." She turned to face his stormy expression.

"The end?" he boomed.

"It's been fun, but we agreed that time would run out. The snow has stopped. It's time to return to reality."

"Which is what, in your opinion?" He sounded as angry as he looked.

She licked her lips and forced out a version of the truth she used to believe. A version before she'd been sealed inside a bubble with a Chase who was both like and unlike the Chase of her memory. He was realer, better, more grown-up. More stable in his life and more solid about his decisions. But she couldn't trust in what she'd learned over the past few days, could she? She had to trust in the ten years separating them and the lesson she'd learned during that time.

"Reality is you in your world and me in mine. *Separately.* It's you in your political career. It's me in my position at MCS." She shrugged, hoping to unshoulder her hectic, confusing emotions. No such luck. "It's time for me to leave. You know it. I know it."

"You don't know what I know, Mimi." He returned his hands to her hips, more intimate now that they stood chest to chest.

"Oh? And what do you think you know?" She shouldn't ask, but couldn't help herself.

"My mother was wrong. She thought you were stubborn and headstrong. She said you were blindly in love with the idea of who I would become. She saw a woman who wanted me for my wallet."

Even though his mother wasn't a part of her life, that hurt.

"I never saw you as any of those things," he continued, his tone softer. Gentler. "You were carefree. Independent. And not because you were trying to be. You just were. *Are*," he corrected.

Some of the stiffness went out of her shoulders.

"When I drove you to the airport and put you on a plane back to Bigfork it wasn't because I agreed with my mother. It was because I agreed with you—agreed that we had a future."

"You did?"

"I did." His voice was low, like admitting it hurt him as much as it hurt her to hear. "I knew you would've moved to Texas, because the stage was set for my future. And because you loved me, you would've come with me."

"I did come with you."

"Don't hide behind glibness." He took a breath. "Maybe my mother was right about you being stubborn, but that's an asset. It was to me…and it is to whomever you choose to share your life with."

She sort of hated how well he knew her. But he did know her. It was as inexplicable now as it was then. As if they were a reincarnated couple who'd already lived out this romance in another time. It was like she knew how it was supposed to end…and they weren't destined to be star-crossed lovers.

"You've grown from an incredibly intelligent, beautiful twenty-three-year-old into an incredibly intelligent, beautiful thirty-three-year-old. Every attribute you possess fits into my life."

Wait. What?

He released her hips and straightened away from her. Away rather than toward, the opposite direction his words had suggested.

"Years ago, I sent you away not because I didn't think you were an incredible woman, and not because my mother is a puppet master. I did it to protect you. From all the things you couldn't protect yourself from. You would've done anything for me—to your own detriment. That's how much you cared."

It was as honest a statement as either of them had made since their reunion.

"I wanted you to know that before you left." He jutted a thumb toward her bedroom door. "I'm going to eat. Join me?"

"All I do is eat." Her teeth found her bottom lip. "Well, not all."

"No. Not all." He smiled from the doorway, but didn't come to her to seal his comment with a kiss. His distance felt wrong, as wrong as what he said next. "I won't bother you any more while I'm in Bigfork."

"Clean break?" she asked, lobbing his words from ten years ago back at him. She half expected an argument. Or maybe she wanted one.

"The cleanest." He dipped his chin in agreement.

With that, the conversation ended. A conversation

so filled with unexplored topics she'd lost count. But one thing was clear.

Their time was up.

Nineteen

"It's Blake," Emmett said when he answered his phone.

"Blake Eastwood? The same guy who Stef—"

"Yes." Emmett cut him off like he couldn't stand to hear the end of that sentence.

On that count, Emmett and Chase agreed. Chase had always appreciated his best friend's surge of protectiveness where his sister was concerned. Blake Eastwood had better steer a wide berth around Stefanie if he wanted to live a long, healthy life with his balls still attached to his person.

"The rat is in-house. One of the campaign interns. Blake targeted her. She's young, pretty. His type."

Chase could practically hear the steam coming out of Emmett's ears.

"She broke into your desk, stole the photo and delivered it to Blake, who's backing your opponent financially," Emmett said. "I questioned her and she burst into tears and confessed that she'd slept with Blake after meeting him in a bar. She didn't know who he was and she definitely did not expect him to blackmail her."

"What a dick."

"He's not done yet. The intern told me before she quit that he said he was planning on staying on top of your new relationship until he hit pay dirt."

Now the steam was mostly coming from Chase's collar. He felt his face heat.

"We went through the rest of our staff with a fine-toothed comb. She's the only defector."

"Thanks, Emmett."

"Things are...good?" The pronounced pause was a clue that he wasn't asking about politics.

"Mimi went home an hour ago. We're no longer snowed in." He'd learned that the best answer was an answer that didn't commit to a direction. *Just the facts.*

Chase had walked her into the garage and held her truck's door for her while she climbed in. Before he could think better of it, and before she could stop him from doing it, he leaned in and kissed her goodbye. Her eyelids were still closed when he backed away and it took everything in him to honor her request for a "clean break" and not make love to her on the front seat of her truck. It was too soon for a goodbye. He'd just found her again, dammit.

"Are you staying in Bigfork?"

"Just until things settle down. Mimi doesn't believe this will disrupt her life. She's wrong."

"Uh-huh." His best friend's tone took on the rare quality of amused. "Not because you wanna stay close?"

More that than the other, but Chase didn't admit as much. He ended the conversation with, "Call me if anything changes" and received Emmett's typical sign-off.

"You got it, boss."

When Miriam had returned home yesterday, there were no waiting paparazzi on her front stoop. And when she drove to work the next morning, she hadn't been chased by a dark car with a long camera lens aimed out the window. Either Chase had overestimated her importance in his opponent's smear campaign, or he'd simply overreacted. Either worked for her. She would prefer to avoid any more drama if possible.

Yesterday she'd driven away from his mansion, his kiss still burning her lips. If he hadn't pulled away— if he hadn't been the one to shut her truck door, she might've been tempted to leap out and pin him to the nearest wall.

That was the effect he had on her. Beyond attraction, his pull was more like gravity. She was the anvil dropped off a cliff. And like gravity wouldn't bear the brunt force of that fall, neither had Chase when she'd followed him home to Dallas ten years ago.

She'd do well remembering that.

On the way to her office inside the main MCS building, she encountered Darren, a fifteen-year-old smarty-pants who practically lived there. He'd started volunteering last summer and had quickly taken a shine to her. She could tell by the way he stuttered her name and watched his shoes whenever he talked to her.

He fidgeted, one tennis shoe scuffing the side of the other as she approached her office.

"Hey, Dare."

"Hi M-Miss Andrix." His smile flinched. "I wanted to talk to you."

"I have a few minutes." She unlocked her door and pushed it open, gesturing for him to go in. "About what?"

"You're in the news."

She dropped her purse and bag onto the desktop. He was talking about the article that'd run about her. Chase had sent her the link yesterday and she'd read it, both unimpressed by how little the author knew about her and frustrated that their relationship had been scandalized.

Flirting with disaster? the tag line had read.

If Chase could ignore it, so could she.

"It's not the news, Darren," she said, but accepted his cell phone anyway. She frowned. The article on the screen wasn't the one she'd read.

"What is this?" she asked rhetorically. The blogger called herself The Dallas Duchess. It seemed the so-called duchess had been granted access to those sneakily snapped photos in Chase's driveway. There were three, one of Chase outside on the phone and glaring, and since he was in protective mode over Mimi, she found that glare disturbingly sexy. Another photo showed him pulling her away from the door. The lead photo captured her own wide eyes and slackened jaw—easily misconstrued as guilt—while Chase stood behind her, jaw set and eyes narrowed.

Mayor Chase Ferguson Stokes an Old Flame.

She wedged her teeth together, uncomfortable with the adjective *old* but she refused to give this the reaction that was warranted. Which, by Miriam's estimations, involved writing a lengthy letter of response to the so-called duchess with explicitly detailed instructions on how to extract her head from her backside.

Miriam handed back the phone and gave Darren an amiable smile. "Thanks for telling me."

"Don't you want to read the article, M-Miss Andrix?"

"No, thank you, Darren. I'm sure it's packed with lies. You shouldn't give them the hits on their website." She winked to let him know she wasn't upset, even though she was. What an antiquated idea to blame the woman for a man's demise.

"It says that you and Chase had a wild affair ten years ago and that you're pulling him into your clutches again." Darren cleared his throat and read from the article. "'Her sights set on Chase's billions to forward her own causes, Miriam—'" he glanced up briefly "—sorry, I mean, M-Miss Andrix 'plans on keeping our mayor on the hook until she bends him to her will. The duchess has always been a fan of the Fergusons, and in this egregious case I'm firmly Team Chase. Miriam—'" Darren mumbled another apology for using her first name "'—if you're reading, leave our beloved mayor alone and find someone in your own hometown to manipulate.'"

"What the hell?" Losing her facade of calm, she snatched Darren's phone and scanned the article for more damning accusations. She found plenty. It went on about how Chase was "unbribable" when it came to money but Miriam wasn't above "using sexual favors to ensnare him." There was even mention of ten years ago and how she'd tried to fit into his life in Dallas but it hadn't worked out.

So. Not an article pitting Chase and Miriam against the world, but rather one in his defense, against the trollop who had "ensnared" him. This blog wasn't antiquated. It was prehistoric.

Numb, Miriam returned his phone and mumbled an apology. Darren offered to avenge her honor by leaving a firmly worded comment on the blog, which was sweet, but she declined.

"Thanks for letting me know," she repeated, this time walking him to her office door. She spared a smile through the crack before shutting him out.

Okay, so Chase *hadn't* been overreacting. She palmed her own cell phone and shakily dialed his number.

"Mimi."

"Our photos are on the Dallas Duchess's blog."

"I know."

"You know?"

"Yes. Emmett called me this morning. I didn't think word would reach you so soon."

"You can thank my secret admirer."

"Who's that?" His stiff tone made her smile.

"He's fifteen. Has asthma. Stutters my name." She liked that Chase sounded slightly jealous, even though she shouldn't. "Did you read it?"

"Yes."

"How does anyone other than our friends and families know we were together that summer?"

"Hard to say. Someone could have called your acquaintances, or your former workplace. It's not as hard to uncover paychecks and flight records as you'd think."

Apparently not.

"Did you…stay in Bigfork?" She sat in her chair in case his answer was yes. Somehow it was easier to stomach if he wasn't close by.

"I stayed." There was a pause during which her heart skipped a beat. "Try not to let the blog bother you. My team is handling it. We'll have this buried soon enough."

"Okay, thanks."

"You're welcome."

An hour later, a sharp knock at her office door preceded her boss Nancy walking in. "Miriam, we need to talk."

Nancy's iPad was in her hand and when she flashed Miriam the screen, on it was the purple-and-gold Dallas Duchess banner.

Chase hadn't lied when he'd told Miriam that his staff was handling things, but that didn't mean he wasn't involved.

As calm as he'd tried to sound to Mimi, he wasn't. He was beyond *pissed*.

At Blake fucking Eastwood for bullying the women in Chase's life. At the Dallas Duchess for stooping to such gossipy lows and making Mimi out to be the enemy.

The first phone call he'd made when he found out was to Zach's wife, Penelope, PR guru.

"I thought the duchess was a friend of yours," he grumbled after she answered.

"I saw it. It's ugly."

His niece cooed in the background and Pen shushed her.

"Sorry." In his rage over Mimi being attacked, he'd checked his manners at the door. Pen was his sister-in-law, the mother of his niece Olivia first. He had no right to bark at her like one of his staff no matter how sour his mood. "I can call at a better time."

"No, it's fine. The nanny is here. I'm just kissing Livvie goodbye before I step into my office." There was a brief conversation with her sitter and then Pen said, "I'm firing up my computer as we speak. Stay on the line." She talked while she typed, outlining a plan to swing the spotlight away from Mimi and over to him.

"Maybe I'll pay Blake a visit," he said, practically spitting his name. "Break a kneecap or two."

"No." Pen laughed. "Absolutely not."

He had to smile. Penelope handled a great many powerful clients with ease. She routinely put billionaires in their places. It was why Chase had entrusted her to untangle Stef and Blake after that mess a year ago. This wasn't the same situation, but it felt eerily similar. A woman he cared about was being manipulated by a douchebag who was chasing his own personal and political gains.

"I was kidding about the knees. Calling him and letting him know I'm onto him would be satisfying."

"He'll record it and then we'll have a bigger mess

on our hands." He liked the way she'd said *we*, including herself in the equation. It's what made her remarkable at her job. Pen cared enough to jump in and get her hands dirty with her clients.

"Won't that help?" he asked. "I'll make sure to point out that Mimi's a victim of his hapless plan."

"That'd be great," Pen's voice resonated with sarcasm. "The press would *love* to spin that as you, a powerful political figure, taking advantage of her like the misogynistic chauvinist you are."

He frowned. He hadn't thought of that.

"Not to mention the Twitter explosion to follow."

"Twitter?"

"Mmm-hmm. Women accusing you of mansplaining to them how the world should work, when you're not arguing how women are too unstable to be involved in politics."

"Man-whatting?" *What the hell?* "I don't think any of those things."

"I know." Her tone was patient. "Trust me, Chase. It's going to get uglier if you defend her."

"I can't let him do this to her." He wouldn't allow her to be harassed. What if this incident put her job in jeopardy? For all he knew, her coworkers might see this as her bedding the enemy. That was the tack the duchess had taken, only in his favor.

"They're already doing it, Chase. If they found more ammunition to use against her, they'll likely sit on it and wait for the perfect moment to drop the bomb. This isn't your first term. You *know* this."

"It's a looming issue until the election," he agreed miserably.

"Is your fear that her reputation will suffer…" A

pause. "Or that you won't win her back now that she's seen the cost of staying with you?"

Was he that transparent?

"I want what's best for her. I'm not it." So much silence came from the other end of the phone that he added, "Hello?"

"You don't think you're good enough for her?" Pen asked.

"I didn't exactly say that."

"What happened in that mansion? What happened between you and Mimi? How much of what the Dallas Duchess reported is true?"

"None of what she said is true. The exact opposite is true."

"Meaning?" Pen wasn't letting this go.

"She's not trying to get her hooks into me. If it was up to me, I'd keep her as close as possible. She's...not interested. In me. Long-term." And who could blame her? Mimi had already received a small dose of what it was like to be with Mayor Chase Ferguson.

"You're interested in a future with her." It wasn't a question, so he didn't answer.

"An upcoming political campaign is not the time to start a new relationship. Or rekindle an old one," he mumbled, hoping Pen's pragmatism would have her agreeing with him.

"That doesn't mean it can't be done."

Well. Hell.

"Don't look for something that's not there," he warned.

A few taps of her keyboard later, Pen said, "I'm looking at the blog and these photos are...well, they

could be anything but now that we've talked I can
see it."

"See what?" He tightened the grip on his phone
and stared out the window at the snowy lake below.

"How protective you are of Mimi. And the tender vulnerability in her that you're trying to protect."

He opened his mouth to protest but he couldn't lie
to Penelope, or himself, any longer.

"Have you told her how you feel?"

"I told her I'd never drag her into the world of politics and oil, yes."

"Chase."

"Penelope."

She sighed, conceding this round. "Sometimes…
headstrong women don't do what's best because we're
trying to make our hearts as firm as our minds. *Sometimes* we need to know what's going on in your heads
and hearts so that we can make the right decision."

"Trust me, Pen. Where Mimi and I are concerned,
the decisions that have been made are the right ones.
Take care of this and there's a bonus in it for you."

"Oh goody," she murmured, droll.

"I'll buy Olivia a pony."

Her laughter chimed, lightening the intensity between them. He could always count on the mention
of Olivia to snap Pen out of work mode. An unfair
tactic, sure, but necessary.

"I'm on it. And, Mr. Mayor?"

"Yes?"

"Don't make the decision for her. Either way."

He nodded even though she couldn't see him, and
then heard a soft click as she signed off.

He hadn't decided anything for Mimi. *She'd* decided. She was the one who was trying to keep her distance. He was carrying out her wishes.

Wasn't he?

Twenty

Miriam was torn between eating or drinking her feelings.

She opened the freezer and eyed a pint of salted caramel ice cream, then closed it and opened the fridge to consider the bottle of prosecco sitting on the top shelf. Prosecco was for celebrating, and she sure as hell didn't feel like doing that, so ice cream it was.

Her phone flashed again—she'd turned off the ringer—and warily she peeked at the screen. "Unknown numbers" had been calling over the last couple of days. She'd ignored them thinking they were sales calls, but after the fifteenth one she'd begun to suspect they had to do with the current surge of blogs written about her and the mayor of Dallas.

Luckily, this number she recognized. Kristine.

"Kris, hi." Miriam dug a spoon out of the drawer

and tossed the lid of the ice cream container into the sink. No need for a bowl tonight. She was bottoming this baby out. "What's new?"

"You mean besides multiple calls from strangers asking me about you and Chase?"

"Ugh. I'm sorry." Heavily, Miriam sat on a kitchen chair.

"You warned me. I'm telling them nothing."

"Thanks, Kris." It'd been two days since Nancy had suggested Miriam take a leave of absence. Word had traveled fast—and not just to her fifteen-year-old admirer Darren. One of the heads of MCS was uncomfortable with the news breaking about her "affair with a mayor." It was an ugly way to paint it, but technically it was true. Nancy worked out a paid leave, but to Miriam, being asked to leave still felt unfair.

"Are you okay otherwise?" Kris asked.

"Other than my phone ringing off the hook with questions about the mayor of Dallas?" She turned her head to the kitchen window. "At least there aren't reporters camped out in my apartment complex."

"It'll blow over, I'm sure. When's the election?"

"A year and a half from now," Miriam announced glumly. Then she blinked when a blur of movement caught her eye. Chase was walking up the sidewalk, head down, collar on his dark coat pulled up. "I have to go. He's here."

"He's there? Meems—"

"I'll call you later." She hung up, no time to talk about how she felt about Chase while he was rapidly approaching her doorway. She slid across her linoleum on slipper socks en route to the living room to check her reflection in the mirror above the couch.

She quickly arranged her hair and checked her teeth, but there wasn't any time to change her clothes. He'd have to see her in a pair of gray leggings and an oversize blue sweatshirt.

The knock came and her eyes sank shut. This was it. And she *really* wasn't ready to see him again.

She yanked open the door and pasted on a smile. "Chase."

"Hi." His shoulders were wedged under his ears, his face red from the walk through the cold.

"Come in." She stepped back and let him in, wondering how a billionaire would view her tiny apartment. If he'd judge her rattling refrigerator or her hand-me-down kitchen table and chairs.

"I called."

She closed the door, noting how much space Chase took up in her itty-bitty kitchen. He dominated the area with his height and his piney scent. She admired how handsome he was with a touch of pain in her chest, his eyes gray against his charcoal wool coat and dark stylishly messy hair.

God. She'd missed him. She hadn't missed him for years, and now two days of being away from him had left a hole in her chest.

If she'd had time on the phone with Kris, Miriam would have admitted she'd partaken of the forbidden fruit and slept with him, but she also would've stated that her only interest in him now revolved around handling the political situation. With him standing in front of her looking strong and like someone she'd like to hold and kiss—and strip naked—Miriam's heart lurched. He wasn't so easily categorized in person.

"Is your phone off?" He was looking around the

room and spotted her pint of ice cream on the table. He canted his head. "Are you all right?"

"I'm on a leave of absence."

"I know. I tried your work first. Nancy answered her phone." His mouth lifted in a teasing tilt.

"I turned my ringer off. It rings constantly."

He pulled in a deep breath. "I'm sorry."

"It's not your fault I protested Big Oil three years ago." She didn't blame him for Blake. The man had no scruples and was trying to get his way at any cost.

"Zach married a woman in public relations. Penelope Brand, now Ferguson," Chase said. "She's handling this on her end. I came over to pass along her phone number so you could touch base and work out a plan. She's the best."

"If it was a Dallas number, I ignored it." She gave him a wan smile and accepted Penelope's business card.

"Understandable."

"Can I get you—" she said at the same time Chase spoke.

"I'm flying out today."

She blinked. "Oh."

"I can handle everything better from home base." He looked to the window and then back at her. "I didn't only come to drop off the business card."

Her breath stalled.

"I didn't want to leave without saying goodbye."

A familiar fault line in her heart shook. Made sense. That break never had healed properly. He came to say goodbye, which was sweet, except that it also meant he was leaving. It was what she wanted. Or, it was what she'd *told* herself she wanted, anyway.

"Do you have everything you need, Mimi?" His words were measured like he expected her to protest.

She gave a jerky nod. She didn't have everything she needed, but she wasn't sure how to voice the unthinkable.

His eyes warmed and he stepped closer. She put out a hand to stop his advance, but when her palm met his chest she smoothed over the thick cotton of his sweater instead. So big and strong and for a few stolen days, hers again.

"Are you sure?" He lowered his lips to her forehead and let out a harsh breath. "There's nothing I'm forgetting before I go?"

Her nose tingled, her eyes heated, but she refused to cry in front of him. And she wouldn't prolong the inevitable.

"I'm good," she lied.

"You're better than good, sweetheart." He pressed his lips to her temple. A shudder shook her spine. It was taking everything in her not to press against him and bury her nose in his neck. "If you need anything… call Penelope, okay?"

It wasn't what she wanted him to say. Wasn't he the one who promised she could call *him* if she needed anything? Had she expected him to come here and make one last profession?

Like what? That now that his political career is suffering a blow, he'd like to marry you?

"What time's your flight?" she asked, the insane thought about marriage lingering in the forefront of her mind. She needed him to leave—for both their sakes.

"Sooner than I'd like." He offered a tender smile. "Why? Need help finishing your ice cream?"

She pulled her fingers down his sweater and stopped on his belt, brushing the cool metal with her thumb. No matter how much she reminded herself that he was no good for her, she went back like an addict who couldn't kick a habit.

When her eyes flicked up to his, it was to witness heat blooming in his darkening pupils. He dipped his head and kissed her hard, pushing her back until her ass hit the kitchen wall. His hands caught her face as he blanketed her with his weight, pressing the length of his body—and the length of his hard-on—against her. She sighed into his mouth, wanting him in spite of how stupid it would be to give in to the throbbing longing in her veins, the merciless pleading of her heart. He felt too good—being near him felt too good.

"Don't go," she whispered.

"Mimi." His lips were off hers, coasting along her cheek. "Honey, I have to go." He let out a dry laugh but when he pulled away she saw the lack of humor in his smile. "God, I have to."

He pulled his hands from her body and pushed them into his hair, leaving her sagging against the wall, her shirt wrinkled, her panties damp. He looked at the ceiling as if gathering his strength and then dropped his arms and met her eyes again.

"What do you want?" he asked evenly.

Wasn't it obvious? Him. Naked. Now.

"Long-term. What do you want?" he reiterated. "A family? A career? A mansion?"

Her hormone-saturated brain slogged through possible answers.

"I need to know, Mimi."

"I want…yeah, a career. I want to teach and work with kids and make the environment better. I don't need a mansion." She gestured at her place. "This is fine. And I have a family. A wonderful family."

His returning nod was solemn. "Good. That's good."

"What do you want?" she asked in return, trying to decipher what he wasn't saying.

"I want to be the mayor of Dallas. I want more nieces, or a nephew. I like my mansion." His smile was lopsided, if not a little sad.

Tears burned behind her eyeballs but she refused to let them fall. The question was asked—a question they'd asked several times over in many different ways.

What did they want?

Chase wanted his life the way it was. Miriam wanted hers the way it was.

No matter how much they wanted each other, that barrier wasn't going anywhere.

"Have a safe flight." She cleared her throat when the words came out tight with emotion. She had to let him go. For the last time. "I guess it'll be a while before you return to Montana, huh?"

His smile faltered. "A little while."

"You'll be reelected, Chase. I'm certain of it."

"And you—" he moved a stray curl from her eye "—will be reinstated to MCS. I'll make sure of it."

"Don't do…whatever it is you're thinking of doing. It's my job. I'll handle it."

"It's my fault you're not there." Before she could

argue, he stole one last kiss. It was far too brief. "Goodbye, Mimi."

"Goodbye, Chase."

He turned for the door without looking back.

And she didn't watch him go.

On the flight to Dallas, Chase watched out the window as clouds passed under the belly of the private jet. He'd taken Pen's advice and asked Mimi what she wanted. He'd given her the chance to say…well, whatever she wanted. Whatever she was brave enough to tell him.

What Mimi had told him was what he should have expected. She wanted to work at Montana Conservation Society and shape the youth of tomorrow. But more than what she *had* said was what she hadn't said.

A speech from ten years ago played in his head.

Back then she hadn't minced a single word. She'd plainly told him they were destined to be together. That they could weather any storm—be it geography or finances or the disapproval of either of their families. She'd mentioned them getting married, an idea that hadn't sounded as horrible to him as he knew it should've. She insisted she'd make a great lawyer's wife, and mentioned how handy—if she ever had to sue someone—it would be to have someone as smart and brave as him on her side.

"We can weather any storm," he mumbled to the window. And yet the literal storm they'd weathered— the blizzard that brought them back together—had been the very thing to drive them apart.

He swiped his face, tired from not sleeping. He'd sat up with a glass of wine or lain and stared at the ceiling over the last two nights, at a loss for what to offer her. The only answer he came up with in those dark, silent hours was to give her what he owed her. Her life back.

Emmett returned to the cabin holding a pair of rocks glasses with a couple of inches of amber-colored liquid in each. "Scotch?"

"If I say no, will you drink both?" Chase asked. One o'clock was early for a nip, but what the hell. Maybe it'd numb the pain that was a permanent resident of his chest.

"Looks like you're the one who needs both." Emmett had insisted on flying out. Said they could make a plan on the flight home for the "situation" in Dallas.

Emmett lowered his big body into the seat across from Chase, eyebrows raised in question.

"It was always a long shot," Chase said, accepting a glass.

"What? You becoming mayor?" Emmett smirked.

"Mimi. She and I…it was never a sure thing."

"Sex muddies the mind," Emmett crossed one leg ankle-to-knee and leaned back. "Creates bonds where there shouldn't be any."

"How the hell do you know?" Chase sipped his scotch and relished the burn low in his throat. "You haven't bonded with any woman you've taken to bed, have you?"

"I wasn't talking about me." Emmett drank from his own glass, peering over the rim at Chase.

"Mimi and I aren't the same. Never have been. Us together…" He searched for the right words. "We hold each other back."

"You hold back." It was a statement that sounded an

awful lot like the start of an argument. "*You're* careful. You heed warning signals. It makes you a great
politician. They had to dig up a woman from ten years
ago to find a scrape of dirt on you." Emmett shook
his head. "Careful's good for your career. Not sure if
it's good everywhere else."

"I'm not going to force her into something she
doesn't want." Namely, him. And his messy life.

"Did you ask her what she wanted?"

"Yes." He was somewhat vindicated that he could
answer honestly.

"No overlaps? No common denominator?"

Chase shook his head though he wasn't sure if
that was true. Sure, their careers were in different
states, but was that insurmountable? No, he realized.
It wasn't. He could have negotiated…he just hadn't.
There were too many reasons not to, at least that's
what he'd convinced himself.

Emmett polished off his drink and stood for a refill.

"Dammit, Em. Are you my advisor or not? What
are you trying to say? Out with it."

Emmett swirled the remaining ice cube in his glass
before raising his face. "Do you love her as much as
you loved her ten years ago?"

Grinding his back teeth together, Chase said, "No."

His friend's expression tightened.

"More." Chase drained his own glass in one gulp.
"I love her more."

"And did you tell her that?"

Chase shook his head.

"Told you. Too careful."

Chase didn't know what he hated more, admitting

to himself that he'd been too chickenshit to tell Mimi the truth, or admitting that his best friend was right.

He *had* been too careful.

But that didn't mean he was too late.

Twenty-One

That afternoon when Stefanie had followed Emmett to Chase's office, she'd learned plenty about what was going on with her oldest brother.

It'd taken some doing, but she'd eventually pried out of Emmett that all of this was over the girl Chase had met when they'd summer vacationed in Montana.

The rebellious age of nineteen at the time, she'd been *not at all* interested in her brother's love life. Not that she was interested in it now, but she was a grown woman and well aware that since he'd returned to Dallas, something was amiss.

When Stef showed up at the conference hall, she flashed a smile at the security guy posted at the door. Since he was one of Emmett's heavies, he knew her—no need to show her credentials. Inside, she bypassed the drooling, hunching horde of reporters, refusing to look any of them in their beady eyes.

Vultures.

As a Ferguson and a billionaire by her own rights, she'd had her fair share of having her name besmirched at any convenient occasion. She had no love for these people. Zero.

She slipped behind the stage and into an adjoining room acting as Chase's hideaway. He looked more tired than usual, but there was a resolute set to his shoulders.

"I have no idea why you cater to those vultures when they're more than happy to tear you into pieces," she told him, folding her arms over her chest.

"Those *vultures* are responsible for my career."

She didn't agree with that, but any arguments on the matter had been trotted out in the past and had always ended with agreeing to disagree.

"Are you okay?" she asked, knowing that he'd likely keep the truth from her on that count, as well.

"Fine."

"I mean it." She put her hand on his shoulder. He looked up from his speech notes, decorated in red ink courtesy of the pen in his hand. "I can't escape the idea that Blake Eastwood's involvement is my fault."

He frowned. "None of this is your fault, Stefanie. It's important for you to understand that."

"It'd feel like a lot less my fault if I didn't know Blake." She added a silent *biblically*, because no matter how grown-up she was, she wasn't willing to discuss sex with her brother.

Chase straightened from his lean against a cheap

desk the room had been outfitted with, and dropped his notes and pen onto it.

"Listen to me," he said. "That bastard would do anything to get to our family. The only mistake you made was trusting him." He palmed her cheek in a rare act of tenderness between them. "I should apologize to you. He took advantage of you, and you're worth more than being a pawn in a vendetta he has against me."

Gratitude clogging her throat, Stef nodded. Chase dropped his arm and bent to meet her gaze.

"Yes?" he asked.

"Yeah," she agreed.

"All right, then. Now get out so I can prepare a statement. And don't look any of the vultures in the eyes on your way out. It's as good as an invitation to harass you."

She smiled, feeling loved and cared for. Chase was a good brother. Both of her brothers were. But that warm fuzzy was obliterated by the appearance of Emmett Keaton, who was the *opposite* of a warm fuzzy.

A cold prickly, she thought with a chuckle.

"Excuse me, Lurch, I was just leaving." She smiled sweetly up at Emmett, who remained silent. His lips flinched into a flat line, which meant she'd gotten under his skin.

Her work was done here.

She sidled along the wall, taking her brother's advice to keep her eyes down. The members of the press were busily preparing for Chase's speech, either touching up their makeup, scrolling through their cell phones or practicing their intros.

As God as her witness, if she ever ended up in a

position of power either at Ferguson Oil or as a politician—Ha!—Stef would never call a meeting to defend her actions.

She exited the room, making a beeline for the coffee bar. On her approach she spotted a familiar brunette woman frantically searching the halls while clutching her purse to her shoulder.

"Miriam Andrix?" Stef kept her voice low so as not to draw unnecessary attention, but Miriam heard her and stopped dead in her tracks.

"Remember me? Chase's sister, Stefanie Ferguson." Stef gestured to herself rather than offer a hand since Miriam was regarding her with wide, wary eyes. No doubt the poor woman had been hounded since the story broke about her and Chase.

"Stefanie." Miriam's shoulders relaxed some, her guard dropping. "Nice to see you."

"You, as well. Is… Chase expecting you?" Surely he would've mentioned it, or appeared more nervous… or anticipatory. Something.

"No. He's not." Miriam gave a quick shake of her head.

Interesting.

Stefanie stepped closer. "Why are you in Dallas?"

"Um… Long story."

I bet.

"Lucky for you, I found you first. I know where Chase is, but a burly security guy is blocking the room. I can get you in."

Hope blossomed on Miriam's face—she really was beautiful. Elegant and lithe, with full lips and expressive dark eyes.

"Penelope told me where to find him and about

the press conference." Miriam's mouth curved into a slight smile. "I came, which I'm sure is a terrible idea. Or at least it is for his career."

"Why's that?" Stef leaned in, interested. The reason behind Miriam's presence was too juicy not to pry.

"Stefanie, darling, there you are!" Eleanor Ferguson approached with quick steps. "Am I too late? Did the press conference start without me? Have you seen Penelope?"

Before Stefanie had a chance to answer any of those questions, Eleanor did a double take of Miriam. Stefanie watched as her mother's face drew down in recognition.

Miriam faced her, pulled her shoulders back and addressed her curtly. "Hello, Eleanor."

Definitely, Miriam hadn't thought this through.

By the time she'd arrived at that conclusion, she'd also arrived in Dallas thanks to a hefty sum paid for a private jet so as not to risk being delayed at the airport.

She couldn't afford to delay one more moment. Ten years had been long enough, and then she'd gone and tacked on another week or so for good measure. Every inch of her ached with words unsaid and emotions unexpressed.

Penelope had called yesterday, and since Chase had delivered her phone number personally, Miriam knew to take the call. The other woman had a plan to unravel the "bad press" surrounding them, but Miriam didn't care about her reputation. She only cared about Chase's.

"If he's anything like his brother, my husband," Penelope had told her, "then Chase is not going to take my advice. He wants to call off the hounds, but I advised him not to come to your defense with the press. I'm concerned they'll twist the story and make him the bad guy. I don't want you to worry about that, though. Don't think of me as taking sides where you and Chase are concerned. My job is to preserve *both* your careers and reputations. Everyone's winning."

Miriam liked Penelope's confidence, but she liked more what she'd said about Chase coming to Miriam's defense. Penelope shared details about the press conference and dropped the name of the conference center, though it was more conversational than intentional.

"When the news hits, and videos and Tweets start, we'll be an hour ahead of it," Pen had said. "One of the stipulations for the press members we chose was that they agreed to wait sixty minutes before sharing anything they learn in that room."

Miriam had gone to bed that night, but she hadn't fallen asleep. She'd stared at the ceiling, stealing a glance at her glowing blue alarm clock now and then. First at midnight, then 1:00 a.m., 1:30 a.m., 2:30 a.m. and finally 4:45 a.m., when she'd given up trying to sleep at all.

She couldn't sleep. She couldn't escape the idea that nothing was as it should be. Chase should be in Dallas: of that she was certain. But not without knowing the truth—a truth she hadn't shared when he stood in her kitchen a few days ago.

Sure, she'd told him a partial truth. She wanted to work with kids. She wanted to save the environment. But she let him believe that her future was wrapped up in her job and that none of it involved him.

That couldn't be further from the truth.

In her defense, she hadn't admitted as much to herself until he was thousands of feet in the air and zooming away from her and her beloved home state.

The next morning, after drinking her second cup of coffee, she made the jittery, spontaneous decision to fly to Dallas.

Ten years ago, he'd put her on a plane back to Montana. He'd let her believe that her leaving was what he wanted. Even recently when they were snowed in together, he'd defended his actions by saying it'd been the right thing to do. He believed he'd been chivalrous, that he'd been protecting her, but she didn't think he'd done what he *wanted*.

Miriam had come all this way, to interrupt the press conference in what might be her worst laid plan to date, to give her and Chase one last chance. One of them had to be brave. She didn't know what he'd say, or what the future would bring, but she knew she could find a job "saving the world" anywhere she damned well pleased. Texas was in as much need of environmental love as Montana.

And she was fairly certain that Chase asking "What do you want?" had everything to do with him catering to her wishes, and nothing to do with what *he* actually wanted.

Déjà vu all over again.

Facing his mother now, Miriam straightened her spine and vowed not to let this woman intimidate her. Ten years ago, she'd endured Eleanor's taut words and prim body language not knowing how to respond. But Miriam was stronger now.

"Is Penelope aware you're here?" Eleanor, who endeavored to take control of every situation, asked.

"I'm not here to see Penelope. I'm here to see your son, Chase."

The older woman's eyebrows climbed her smooth forehead. "I know you don't have much political know-how, but surely you're aware that your being here puts his campaign in grave jeopardy."

What Miriam was sure about was that Chase was an amazing man, an amazing politician with amazing friends on his side—one of them a plucky, capable PR maven. He'd come out of this snag just fine. He'd been certain of it, and so was she.

"He's a big boy," Miriam replied. "I'm sure he'll handle whatever fallout occurs from my walking through those doors and saying what I came here to say."

Affronted, Eleanor's jaw dropped. "Stefanie, kindly call hotel security before Miriam causes a ruckus."

"I want to hear what she has to say." Chase's sister flashed a pretty smile, and like that, Miriam became a big, *big* fan of Stefanie Ferguson.

Acting on instincts born of a thirty-three-year-old woman—and far from the headstrong twenty-three-year-old she'd been ten years ago—Miriam reached out and touched Eleanor's arm.

"I don't want this to end with me crying or hating you again. I don't want this to end with me conceding and him staying quiet to keep the peace. I'm going to tell Chase how I feel and let him decide what to do from there."

"How *do* you feel?" Eleanor's voice was coated in shock, or maybe denial. Miriam wasn't sure the woman really wanted to know, but she'd asked, so here went nothing.

"I loved him ten years ago. I wanted nothing more than to be at his side for the rest of our lives. I never thought I'd see him again. He's the one who came back to Montana—who bought the mansion above the beach where we used to trespass and skinny-dip."

Eleanor paled, but Miriam wasn't through yet.

"I was the one who showed up on his doorstep with sweet potato pie, but make no mistake, Eleanor. Chase is the one who came back."

He'd pursued her under the guise of getting her back into his bed. Under the guise, she suspected, of proving to himself that he was over her. But the conclusion she'd arrived at that sleepless night was that he'd needed that guise. It was the safest path out of Montana and back to Dallas. To his destiny, and leaving her to hers.

"I never expected to fall in love with him again," she confessed. "In a way I guess I didn't. I think I never fell out, and those dormant feelings were jarred awake when I spent Thanksgiving weekend with him. I know you don't think I'm good for Chase, but I don't care what you think. We were too careful the first time around. I'm not going to make the same mistake this time."

An excited squeal came from over her shoulder. Miriam turned to find Stefanie cupping her mouth with both hands and bouncing on the balls of her feet.

"Sorry," she parted her hands to say. "I'm sorry. This is so exciting." She raised her eyebrows and grinned at her mother.

Eleanor's expression was more downtrodden and

tired then argumentative. That was certainly a surprise. Miriam remembered the older woman's words being formed of steel wool. No doubt a similar speech lingered at the base of Eleanor's throat about how Miriam and Chase were too young or would never make it, or about how Miriam would ruin his reputation. Or… maybe not? Maybe Eleanor had learned something over the last decade, as well.

Chase's mother scanned Miriam's attire, a simple black dress, high heels and long coat. Miriam gripped her Coach purse, the only nice handbag she owned, and bore the older woman's scrutiny.

"You're serious," Eleanor concluded. "You love Chase in a real and lasting way."

Miriam shook her head, but not in denial. "*Real* is the only way I know how to love him."

Twenty-Two

Without introduction, Chase stepped onto the stage in the conference room. A hush fell over the invited members of the press, and he squinted against the hot lights over the podium.

Pen had advised him on how to handle questions about Mimi. She'd reminded him again on the Post-It note attached to his speech that arrived by courier just twenty minutes ago. Red ink decorated the edges of the notes—his changes—including the X he'd drawn over Pen's Post-it note suggestion. His sister-in-law wasn't going to like what he'd say, but he'd ignored advice before to cater to his own gut call.

Today was one of those days.

"Thank you for coming out today at my office's request," he started. Cameras flashed and pens were set at the ready on notepads. "As you're aware, I've been recently accused of involvement with a woman who has ties to environmentalist groups. Groups that stand against entities like Ferguson Oil. I was involved with this woman ten years ago, over a summer spent in Bigfork, Montana. Our relationship predated my political career, and though she'd vocalized her distaste for my family's industry at the time, she didn't hold it against me."

He couldn't help smiling at the memory of when he'd broken the news. Miriam had looked politely appalled, and then resigned. She'd rolled her eyes and said something to the effect of *Good thing I love you*.

Chase folded his notes and set them aside. The rest of what he had to say wasn't going to be read from his prepared speech.

"A good friend of mine dispensed some valuable advice recently. The kind of advice you don't want to hear, but he tells you anyway."

Emmett was keeping an eye on the crowd, but Chase made out the slightest half smile on his friend's profile.

"He told me I was too careful." Chase pulled in a breath of pure will. Admitting he was wrong had never been a strength. "My friend was right. I am careful. Service has long been my role. My function. As the first-born son of the Fergusons, my destiny is to serve my family and my voters and our shared business. I can't afford to serve myself. Or..." The next vulnerable admission required a brief pause before he decided to hell with it. "Or my heart."

Gasps rose in the crowd, one notably from his mother who just entered the room. Good. She, especially, needed to hear this.

"As the slander continues from my opponent's team, I'm faced with my past and the unfair way it's being portrayed. I don't care what dirt you find on me from that summer ten years ago. I only care about how you treat Miriam Andrix."

He paused to let that sink in as his sister slipped in behind his mother. Then he focused on the crowd of reporters in the front row who eagerly scribbled onto notepads or pecked notes into their phones. Cameras with bright lights closed in to capture his face during this truth-telling debacle—something Penelope Ferguson would reprimand him for, he was sure.

He held up the papers he'd set aside. "This speech would have me confessing that I was young and foolish years ago. That I followed my heart and not my head, and as a result became entangled with a woman who wasn't destined to become my future. I've always known who to serve, and in what order. My family. The great city of Dallas. My family's business. Breaking things off with Miriam was the right thing to do for my career and for her. I never wanted her to have to deal with scrutiny. I never wanted her under the microscope with me. It's what I signed up for, and nothing she would ever ask for. I've long been in the habit of protecting the ones I love."

Quiet whisperings rose but fell silent again when he continued.

"Miriam Andrix has a big heart and a strong will." He allowed a smile when he pictured her stubbornly standing her ground. "For as long as I've known her, she's been hell-bent on saving the world. An admirable feat since most of us downgrade to simply saving ourselves. I'm not here to admit I was a foolish youth. I'm here to make a request. When I left Bigfork, Montana, I left Miriam to her life and she let me return to mine. Leave her alone. It's past time to refocus the campaign on me and what I can do for our city."

He nodded that he was through and reporters shot out of their seats. Many waved, most called his name.

"Yes, Donna." He pointed at the older gray-haired woman in the second row.

"Mr. Mayor, welcome home. What's the first order of business?"

"You mean besides spending my first day back with you fine people?" He grinned and soft laughter rolled over the crowd. "I'll be in my office, my sights set on Dallas and winning the reelection."

Canned but charming answers were always the best choices.

He pointed at a young intern for the city paper. "Bobby."

"Uh, yes, Mr. Mayor. Will you retaliate against your opponent for trying to slander your good name?"

"We always take the high road, Bobby. You know this."

"Fiona." He pointed at a middle-aged blonde woman.

"Mr. Mayor, will you be returning to Bigfork any time soon?"

"I own a house there, so I'm sure I will return. How soon isn't something I'm comfortable sharing with you yet." He capped that answer with a smile and pointed to a white-haired man. "Tom."

"Mr. Mayor, we've heard you say in the past that the oil industry…"

And so the questions went, the focus back where

it should be: on Chase's company and his position as one of the leaders of the city. Just like he'd asked, and they paid him that respect. After a few more answers, he concluded the conference.

"Now if you'll excuse me, I—"

"Mr. Mayor!" came a shout from the back of the room. The camera lights swept away from him.

Mutterings like "That's her!" and "Miriam! Miriam!" crested like a wave.

He blinked the woman into focus. *Miriam?*

The same woman who'd won his heart…twice. But who was counting?

"Yes. The brunette in the back," Chase said, enamored by her all over again.

"Are you single, Mr. Mayor?" Mimi called out.

"Pitifully so," he said into the microphone. A few of the cameras swung back to him. "As a result of a recent tragic error."

She pushed through the crowd toward him, her smile tentative. "What error was that?"

"I left the woman I was in love with in another state without telling her how I feel."

Mimi stopped moving, her eyes trained on him, her mouth parting softly.

"That *is* tragic," she finally managed.

Murmurings came from the crowd, but no one interrupted.

"If you have time," Mimi said. "I have just one more question."

Chase didn't make it a habit of being thrown off-guard, yet here he was. What was she doing here? Why had she come? But instead of asking, he simply answered her question. "I have time."

"Would you ever again consider dating a woman with a history of protesting the oil industry?"

The hope—the love—on Mimi's face echoed his own so fiercely, the next word was hard to get past his throat.

"No."

Her face fell, and the reporters around her strained closer with microphones and cameras, silent and slack-jawed with curiosity.

"I'd ask her to marry me," Chase said, a smile inching across his face, "but only if she loved me as much as I love her."

In the bright lights, he could make out tears shining on the edges of Mimi's eyelids.

"Do you love me?" he asked, swallowing thickly. Risky, this, but he was now in the risk-taking business.

"I do."

He more read her lips than heard her. His joy over those two words was so overwhelming that he leaped from the stage and rushed through the crowd. Cameras snapped; questions shot like cannons around him. He narrowed his focus on Mimi, kissing her for the world—or at least for Dallas—to see.

Three words echoed in his head as he met her mouth with eagerness.

She loves me. She loves me.

When he pulled away, she was grinning up at him, her arms around his neck.

"Mr. Mayor!" He recognized the voice of Channel 9's premier reporter who'd long been one of his supporters.

"Yes, Phil?"

"Was that a real proposal?"

Chase turned to Mimi who was in his arms, a crease of worry decorating her brow.

"Yes," he told her, his smile permanent.

"What was your answer, Miriam?" Phil asked as the crowd around them quieted.

Mimi's fingers tickled the back of Chase's neck and she tipped her chin. "I could make or break your career, Mayor."

"My career isn't what I'm concerned about. It's me who you're making or breaking."

"I'm more into making." Her smile widened.

He thought of them making out, making love, and decided she was right. She was more into making.

"Very well," she whispered in his ear. "I accept."

Caught up in her and the moment, Chase leaned in to take her lips in another kiss… But not before Fiona interrupted with, "Was that a yes or a no on the marriage proposal?"

"Should we give her the scoop?" Mimi asked against his lips.

"I'll let you do the honors."

"Yes," she turned her head to tell the crowd, and then she stood on her tiptoes and brushed her nose against his. "My answer's always been yes."

* * * * *

When lies about Stefanie Ferguson threaten her
family's reputation, she finds the perfect solution...
and proposes to Emmett Keaton!

Don't miss Stefanie's story in
the next DALLAS BILLIONAIRE'S CLUB *novel*
by Jessica Lemmon!

A CHRISTMAS PROPOSITION

Available December 2018,
wherever Harlequin Desire books are sold!

COMING NEXT MONTH FROM

HARLEQUIN
Desire

Available September 4, 2018

#2611 KEEPING SECRETS
Billionaires and Babies • by Fiona Brand
Billionaire Damon Smith's sexy assistant shared his bed and then vanished for a year. Now she's returned—with his infant daughter! Can he work through the dark secrets Zara's still hiding and claim the family he never knew he wanted?

#2612 RUNAWAY TEMPTATION
Texas Cattleman's Club: Bachelor Auction
by Maureen Child
When Caleb attends a colleague's wedding, the last person he expects to leave with is the runaway bride! He offers Shelby a temporary hideout on his ranch. But soon the sizzle between them has this wealthy cowboy wondering if seduction will convince her to stay...

#2613 STRANGER IN HIS BED
The Masters of Texas • by Lauren Canan
Brooding Texan Wade Masters brings his estranged wife home from the hospital with amnesia. This new, sensual, *kind* Victoria makes him feel things he never has before. But when he discovers the explosive truth, will their second chance at love be as doomed as their first?

#2614 ONE NIGHT SCANDAL
The McNeill Magnates • by Joanne Rock
Actress Hannah must expose the man who hurt her sister. Sexy rancher Brock has clues, but amnesia means he can't remember them—or his one night with her! Still, he pursues her with a focus she can't resist. What happens when he finds out everything?

#2615 THE RELUCTANT HEIR
The Jameson Heirs • by HelenKay Dimon
Old-money heir Carter Jameson has a family who thrives on deceit. He's changing that by finding the woman who knows devastating secrets about his father. The problem? He wants her, maybe more than he wants redemption. And what he thinks she knows is nothing compared to the truth...

#2616 PLAYING MR. RIGHT
Switching Places • by Kat Cantrell
CEO Xavier LeBlanc must resist his new employee—his inheritance is on the line! But there's more to her than meets the eye...because she's working undercover to expose fraud at his charity. Too bad Xavier is falling faster than her secrets are coming to light...

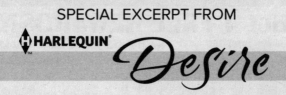
Shelby Arthur stared at her own reflection and hardly
recognized herself. She supposed all brides felt like
that on their wedding day, but for her, the effect was
terrifying.

She was looking at a stranger wearing an old-fashioned
gown with long, lacy sleeves, a cinched waist and full
skirt, and a neckline that was so high she felt as if she
were choking. Shelby was about to get married in a dress
she hated, a veil she didn't want, to a man she wasn't sure
she liked, much less loved. How did she get to this point?

"Oh, God. What am I doing?"

She'd left her home in Chicago to marry Jared
Goodman. But now that he was home in Texas, under
his awful father's thumb, Jared was someone she didn't

even know. Her whirlwind romance had morphed into a nightmare and now she was trapped.

Shelby met her own eyes in the mirror and read the desperation there. In a burst of fury, she ripped her veil off her face. Then, blowing a stray auburn lock from her forehead, she gathered up the skirt of the voluminous gown in both arms and hurried down the hall and toward the nearest exit.

And ran smack into a brick wall.

Well, that was what it felt like.

A tall, gorgeous brick wall who grabbed her upper arms to steady her, then smiled down at her with humor in his eyes. He had enough sex appeal to light up the city of Houston, and the heat from his hands, sliding down her body, made everything inside her jolt into life.

"Aren't you headed the wrong way?" he asked, and the soft drawl in his deep voice awakened a single thought in her mind.

Oh, boy.

Don't miss
Runaway Temptation
by USA TODAY *bestselling author Maureen Child,*
the first in the Texas Cattleman's Club:
Bachelor Auction series.

Available September 2018 wherever
Harlequin® Desire books and ebooks are sold.

www.Harlequin.com

Want to give in to temptation with
steamy tales of irresistible desire?

Check out **Harlequin® Presents®**,
Harlequin® Desire and
Harlequin® Kimani™ Romance books!

New books available every month!

CONNECT WITH US AT:

Harlequin.com/Community

Facebook.com/HarlequinBooks

Twitter.com/HarlequinBooks

Instagram.com/HarlequinBooks

Pinterest.com/HarlequinBooks

ReaderService.com

**ROMANCE WHEN
YOU NEED IT**

PGENRE2017